CW00871810

1 MONTH OF
FREE
READING

at

www.ForgottenBooks.com

By purchasing this book you are eligible for one month membership to ForgottenBooks.com, giving you unlimited access to our entire collection of over 1,000,000 titles via our web site and mobile apps.

To claim your free month visit:

www.forgottenbooks.com/free809431

ISBN 978-0-365-25536-9
PIBN 10809431

SELECT

Recitations and Readings.

ADDED TO WHICH IS THE CHARMING COMEDIETTA,

THE LOAN OF A LOVER.

(FOR SIX CHARACTERS.)

By J. R. PLANCHE,

Author of "THE CAPTAIN OF THE WATCH." ETC.

NEW YORK:

STREET & SMITH, Publishers,

31 Rose Street.

PN4
.S 5

PREFACE.

It has been our aim to have the "SELECT RECITA-
TIONS AND READINGS" not only gems of literary excellence,
but of such pith and meaning, that the verbal construc-
tion of the narrative or description will be as much appre-
ciated as effectiveness of delivery.

Much attention should be paid by readers to the choice
of subjects. Elocutionists of equal merit are not at all
equal in the rendition of certain pieces. A. has his favorite selections, in which he is considered unapproachable;
and B. has his, which he has made almost his own, by his
animation and vividness of illustration. From experience,
or experiments before select audiences, each is aware that
should he encroach upon the other's especial programme,
he would suffer by contrast.

It follows, then, that if a speaker has made a wise selection for the display of his elocutionary talents—a selection
not only suited to his style and ability, but likely to be
intrinsically interesting to his audience—the power to
enunciate distinctly, understandingly, deliberately, and
elucidate the author's meaning with discriminating intona-
tion and emphasis, as well as appropriate gestures, will
make his recitation a success.

To be an entertaining elocutionist, the speaker must
thoroughly comprehend his subject, and be in sympathy

with it; he must *feel* what he portrays, like an able actor, and utter his words with such energy, spirit, and distinctness that they cannot be misunderstood, and with an earnestness certain to command attention.

Reading in public is beneficial in many ways. It gives a young person confidence, so that should occasion arise, he will have courage to address an assemblage; it improves the memory, and inspires a taste for literature; it induces the speaker to closely study the author's meaning—that he may thoroughly appreciate and understand the thought which is merely suggested, but not expressed; it gives command of language, for it must be admitted that the frequent use of elegant diction, the words of the acknowledged masters of literature and eloquence, is certain to make the speaker graceful, fluent, and convincing, not only on the rostrum, but in the ordinary intercourse and conversation of life.

The subjects in the "SELECT RECITATIONS AND READINGS" take a wide scope; they are serious and pleasant, tragic and heroic, droll and pathetic, ranging "from grave to gay, from lively to severe." They comprise some of the productions of the master minds of the world—poets, orators, statesmen and philosophers; and they are adapted for young or old, for parlor entertainments, for school exhibitions, or for public occasions.   T. C. G.

CONTENTS

PAGE.

Advice to a Young Man................Ben Jonson...................171
A Free Seat.................................Anonymous....................134
American Flag............................Joseph Rodman Drake....... 34
Apostrophe to Water....................Judge Arrington............. 10
Battle of Fontenoy......................Thomas Davis.................161
Bivouac of the Dead....................Theodore O'Hara............156
Blind Boy's Speech......................Park Benjamin.............. 76
Cane-Bottomed Chair....................Wm. M. Thackeray...........128
Clown's Baby.............................Margaret Vandegrift.......130
Come Back.................................Bill Nye..................... 11
Dirge For a Soldier.....................George H. Boker............. 89
Drones of the Community...............Percy Bysshe Shelley.........164
Dying Soldier...........................Richard Coe.................105
Field of Waterloo.......................Byron........................102
Filial Piety............................Richard Brinsley Sheridan.. 88
Freshman's Story.........................Max Adeler................... 53
Friend of the Red Man..................Max Adeler................... 7
Gambler's Wife..........................E. R. Coates.................159
Guilt Cannot Keep Its Own Secret.....Daniel Webster............... 14
Hour of Death...........................Felicia Hemans..............112
Housekeeper's Soliloquy...............Mrs. F. D. Gage..............113
How a Man Gets Up in the Morning..Kate Thorn................... 15
Importance of the Union...............Daniel Webster............... 32
Just One................................Azalea E. Osgood............. 57
Katie Lee and Willie Grey..............J. H. Pixley................. 92
Laugh on, Laugh on, To-day...........Winthrop M. Praed.......... 79
Lines on a Skeleton....................Anonymous................... 51
Little Sister of Charity................Francis S. Smith............. 36
Lord of Burleigh........................Alfred Tennyson............. 98
Lost Mother-in-Law.....................Max Adeler..................107
Men to Make a State....................George W. Doane............. 67
Mother and Child........................Nelly B. Simmons............ 70
Mrs. Grubbs' Railroad Claim..........Charles W. Foster............ 25
Nature's Noblemen......................Martin F. Tupper............166
Never Despair...........................Wm. C. Richards.............170
Nothing But Leaves.....................Lucy Evelina Ackerman..... 78

6 CONTENTS.

PAGE.

Ode To My Little Son .... Thomas Hood 59
Old Actor's Story .... George R. Sims. 122
Onward, Onward .... Linnæs Banks 172
Pauper's Death-Bed .... Caroline Bowles Southey 104
Persevere ....: .... John Brougham 90
Procrastination .... Charles Mackay 169
Psalm of Marriage .... Phœbe Cary 119
Rill From the Town Pump .... Nathaniel Hawthorne 72
Ring out the Old Year .... Alfred Tennyson 83
Ruth .... R. K. Munkittrick 49
Santa Claus' Stocking .... Francis S. Smith 84
Sketch of Bonaparte ....: .... Charles Phillips 18
Some Time .... : .... Eugene Field 133
Song of the Camp ... : ....- .... Bayard Taylor 151
Song of the Canteen .... Charles G. Halpine 24
Speak No Ill .... Charles Swain 58
Spiritual Freedon—What is it? .... William Ellery Channing ... 81
St. Leon's Toast .... Walter Scott 136
Surprise Party .... Francis S. Smith 61
Taking Mrs. Jones' Census .... Max Adeler 94
Thanatopsis .... William Cullen Bryant 46
The Bible .... Donoso Cortes 153
The Brave at Home .... T. Buchanan Read 118
The Charity Dinner .... Litchfield Mosely 142
The Cynic .... Henry Ward Beecher 173
The Heavens Declare the Glory of
    God .... Joseph Addison 77
The Hour Glass .... John Quincy Adams 177
The Jiners .... Anonymous 138
The Late Mr. McGlucken .... Max Adeler 21
THE LOAN OF A LOVER .... J. R. Planche 179
The Needle .... Samuel Woodworth 158
The Pilgrims .... Edward Everett 101
The Traitor's Death-Bed .... George Lippard 115
The Two Glasses: .... Ella Wheeler Wilcox 149
The Water Mill .... D. C. McCallum 120
The World For Sale .... Ralph Hoyt 167
Tom's Wife .... W. H. Harrison 152
Tribute to Genius and Labor .... Epes Sargent 176
Tubal Cain .... Charles Mackay 110
War in America .... Earl of Chatham 39
What the Skipper Said .... Max Adeler 42
Yankee Boy .... John Pierpont 175

SELECT
Recitations and Readings.

NUMBER ONE.

A FRIEND OF THE RED MAN.

" I don't take the same view of the North American Indian that most people do," said Professor Trotter, in a discussion down at the grocery store the other night. " Now some think that the red man displays a want of good taste in declining to wash himself; but I don't. What is dirt? It is simply—matter—the same kind of matter that exists everywhere. The earth is made of dirt; the things we eat are dirt, and they grow in the dirt; and when we die and are buried, we return again to the dirt from which we were made. Science says that all dirt is clean. The savage Indian knows this; his original mind grasps this idea; he has his eagle eye on science; and he has no soap. Dirt is warm. A layer one-sixteenth of an inch thick on a man is said by Professor Huxley to be as comfortable as a fifty-dollar suit of clothes. Why then should the child of the forest undress himself once a week by scraping this off, and expose himself to the rude blasts of winter? He has too much sense. His head is too level to let him take a square wash more than once in every two hundred years, and even then he don't rub hard.

"And then in regard to his practice of eating dogs; why shouldn't a man eat a dog? A dog sometimes eats a man, and turn about is fair play. A well-digested dog stowed away on the inside of a Choctaw squaw, does more to advance civilization and the Christian religion than a dog that barks all night in a back yard, and makes people get up out of bed and swear, don't it? And nothing is more nutritious than dog. Professor Huxley says that one pound of a dog's hind leg, nourishes the vital forces more than a wagon load of bread and corned beef. It contains more phosphorus and carbon. When dogs are alive they agree with men, and there is no reason why they shouldn't when they are dead. This nation will enter upon a glorious destiny when it stops raising corn and potatoes, and devotes itself more to growing crops of puppies.

"Now many ignorant people consider scalping inhuman. I don't. I look upon it as one of the most beneficent processes ever introduced for the amelioration of the sufferings of the human race. What is hair? It is an excrescence. If it grows it cost a man a great deal of money and trouble to keep it cut. If it falls out the man becomes bald, and the flies bother him. What does the Indian do in this emergency? With characteristic sagacity he lifts out the whole scalp, and ends the annoyance and expense. And then look at the saving from other sources. Professor Huxley estimates that two thousand pounds of the food that a man eats in a year go to nourish his hair. Remove that hair and you save that much food. If I had my way, I would have every baby scalped when it is vaccinated, as a measure of political economy. That would be statesmanship. I have a notion to organize a political party on the basis of baby-scalping, and to go on the stump to advocate it. If people had any sense, I might run into the Presidency as a baby-scalper.

"And as for the matter of the Indians wearing rings through their noses, I don't see why people complain of that. Look at the advantage it gives a man when he wants to hold on to anything. If a hurricane strikes an Indian, all he does is to hook his nose-ring over a twig of a tree, and there he is, fast and sound. And it gives him something to rest his pipe on when he smokes, while, in the case of a man with a pug, the ring helps to jam his proboscis down, and to make it a Roman nose. But I look at it from a sanitary point of view. The Indian suffers from catarrh. Now what will cure that disease? Metal in the nose in which electricity can be collected. Professor Huxley says that the electricity in a metal ring two inches in diameter will cure more catarrh than all the medicine between here and Kansas. The child of nature with wonderful instinct has perceived this, and he teaches us a lesson. When we, with our higher civilization, begin to throw away finger-rings and ear-rings, and to wear rings in our noses, we will be a hardier race. I am going to direct the attention of Congress to the matter.

"Then take the objections that are urged to the Indian practice of driving a stake through a man, and building a bonfire on his stomach. What is their idea? They want to hold that man down. If they sit on him they would obstruct the view of him. They put a stake through him, and there he is secured by simple means, and if it is driven in carefully, it may do him good. Professor Huxley says that he once knew a man who was cured of yellow jaundice by falling on a pale-fence, and having a sharp-pointed paling run into him. And the bonfire may be equally as healthy. When a man's stomach is out of order, you put a mustard plaster on it. Why? To warm it. The red man has the same idea. He takes a few fagots, lights them, and applies them to the stomach. It is a certain cure. Professor Huxley——"

"Oh, dry up about Professor Huxley!" exclaimed Meigs, the storekeeper, at this juncture.

"Wh-wh-what d' you say?" asked the professor.

"I say, you stop blowing about Professor Huxley, and you'd better shut up any way. I have had enought of gab from you to night."

Then the professor rose sadly, reached over for a cracker, wiped his nose thoughtfully on his sleeve, and sauntered across the street to the bar-room to see if he could find anybody to ask him to take a drink.

MAX ADELER.

APOSTROPHE TO WATER.

In the early days of Texas an invitation had been issued by Paul Denton, a Western missionary, to several of the residents of one of the settlements, to attend a barbecue, and they were promised an abundance of food, and " *the best of liquor.*"

When they came, with the expectation of having a grand carouse, they were amazed to learn that although there was plenty to eat, there was not a drop of liquor. This is the story as narrated in a sketch from the vivid and poetic pen of Judge Arrington, whose *nom de plume* was Charles Summerfield. When the Texans clamored for liquor, Paul Denton burst forth with the appended eloquent apostrophe to water:

Look at that, ye thirsty ones of earth! Behold it! See its purity! See how it glitters, as if a mass of liquid gems! It is a beverage that was brewed by the hand of the Almighty himself. Not in the simmering still or smoking fires, choked with poisonous gases, and surrounded by the stench and sickening odors and rank corruptions, doth our Father in Heaven prepare the precious essence of life, the pure cold water, but in the green glade and glassy dell, where the red deer wanders and the child loves to play! There God brews it, and down, down in the deepest valleys, where the fountains murmur, and the rills sing; and high upon the tall mountain-tops, where the naked granite glitters like gold in the sun; where the storm-clouds brood and the thunder-storms crash; and away out on the billowy sea, where the hurricanes howl music, and the big waves roar the chorus, chanting the march of God—there He brews it, that beverage of life—health-giving water.

And everywhere it is a thing of beauty—gleaming in the dew-drop, singing in the summer rain, shining in the ice-gem, till the trees all seemed turned into living jewels —spreading a golden vail over the setting sun, or a white gauze around the midnight moon—sporting in the catar-act, sleeping in the glaciers, dancing in the hail showers— folding its bright curtain softly about the wintry world, and weaving the many colored iris, that seraph's zone of the sky, whose roof is the sunbeam of heaven, all check-ered over with celestial flowers, by the mystic hand of rarefaction—still always it is beautiful, that blessed life-water! No poison bubbles on the brink! Its foam brings no sadness or murder; no blood-stains in its limpid glass; broken-hearted wives, pale widows, and starving orphans shed no tears in its depths; no drunkard's shrinking ghost, from the grave, curses it in words of eternal despair. Beau-tiful, pure, blessed, and glorious! give me forever the sparkling, cold water!   JUDGE ARRINGTON.

COME BACK.

EDITOR NEW YORK WEEKLY:

Dear Sir:—I wish that you would insert the following personal in your valuable and widely read paper:

PERSONAL—WILL THE YOUNG WOMAN WHO used to cook in our family, and who went away, ten pounds of sugar, and five and a half pounds of tea ahead of the game, please come back, and all will be for-given.

If she cannot return, will she please write, stating her present address, and also give her reasons for shutting up the cat in the refrigerator when she went away?

If she will only return, we will try to forget the past, and think only of the glorious present, and the bright, bright future.

Come back, Sarah, and jerk the waffle-iron for us once more.

Your manners are peculiar, but we yearn for your doughnuts, and your style of streaked cake suits us exactly.

You may keep the handkerchiefs and the collars, and we will not refer to the dead past.

We have arranged it so that when you snore, it will not disturb the night police, and if you do not like our children, we will send them away.

We realize that you do not like children very well, and our children especially gave you much pain because they were not so refined as you were.

We have often wished, for your sake, that we had never had any children; but so long as they are in our family, the neighbors will rather expect us to take care of them.

Still, if you insist upon it, we will send them away. We don't want to seem overbearing with our servants.

· We would be willing, also, to give you more time for mental relaxation than you had before. The intellectual strain incident to the life of one who makes gravy for a lost and undone world must be very great, and tired nature must at last succumb. We do not want you to succumb. If any one has got to succumb, let us do it.

All we ask is that you will let us know when you are going away, and leave the crackers and cheese where we can find them.

It was rather rough on us to have you go away when we had guests in the house, but if you had not taken the key to the cooking department, we could have worried along.

You ought to let us have company at the house sometimes, if we let you have company when you want to. Still, you know best, perhaps. You are older than we are, and you have seen more of the world.

We miss your gentle admonitions, and your stern reproofs sadly. Come back and reprove us again. Come back and admonish us once more, at so much per admonish and groceries.

We will agree to let you select the tender part of the steak, and such fruit as seems to strike you favorably, just as we did before. We did not like it when you were here, but that is because we were young, and did not know what the customs were.

If a life-time devoted to your welfare can obliterate the injustice we have done to you, we will be glad to yield it to you.

If you could suggest a good place for us to send the children, where they would be well taken care of, and where they would not interfere with some other cook who is a friend of yours, we would be glad to have you write us.

My wife says that she hopes you will feel perfectly free to use the piano whenever you are lonely or sad, and when you or the bread feel depressed, you will be welcome to come into the parlor and lean up against either one of us and sob.

We know that when you were with us before, we were a little reserved in our manner toward you, but if you come back it will be different.

We will introduce you to more of our friends this time, and we hope you will do the same by us. Young people are apt to get above their business, and we admit that we were wrong.

Come back and oversee our fritter bureau once more.

Take the portfolio of our interior department.

Try to forget our former coldness.

Return, oh, wanderer, return!   BILL NYE.

GUILT CANNOT KEEP ITS OWN SECRET.

An aged man, without an enemy in the world, in his own house, and in his own bed, is made the victim of a butcherly murder, for mere pay. The fatal blow is given! and the victim passes, without a struggle or a motion, from the repose of sleep to the repose of death! It is the assassin's purpose to make sure work. He explores the wrist for the pulse. He feels for it, and ascertains that it beats no longer! It is accomplished. The deed is done. He retreats, retraces his steps to the window, passes out through it as he came in, and escapes. He has done the murder;—no eye has seen him, no ear has heard him. The *secret* is his own—and it is safe!

Ah! gentlemen, that was a dreadful mistake. Such a secret can be safe nowhere. The whole creation of God has neither nook nor corner where the guilty can bestow it, and say it is safe. Not to speak of that eye which glances through all disguises, and beholds everything as in the splendor of noon, such secrets of guilt are never safe from detection, even by men. True it is, generally speaking, that "murder will out." True it is, that Providence hath so ordained, and doth so govern things, that those who break the great law of Heaven, by shedding man's blood, seldom succeed in avoiding discovery. Especially, in a case exciting so much attention as this, discovery must come, and will come, sooner or later.

A thousand eyes turn at once to explore every man, every thing, every circumstance, connected with the time and place; a thousand ears catch every whisper; a thousand excited minds intensely dwell on the scene, shedding all their light, and ready to kindle the slightest circumstance into a blaze of discovery.

Meantime, the guilty soul cannot keep its own secret. It is false to itself; or, rather, it feels an irresistible impulse of conscience to be true to itself. It labors under its guilty possession, and knows not what to do with it. The human heart was not made for the residence of such an inhabitant. It finds itself preyed on by a torment, which it dares not acknowledge to God or man. A vulture is devouring it, and it can ask no sympathy or assistance, either from Heaven or earth.

The secret which the murderer possesses soon comes to possess him; and, like the evil spirits of which we read, it overcomes him, and leads him whithersoever it will. He feels it beating at his heart, rising to his throat, and demanding disclosure. He thinks the whole world sees it in his face, reads it in his eyes, and almost hears its workings in the very silence of his thoughts. It has become his master. It betrays his discretion, it breaks down his courage, it conquers his prudence.

When suspicions, from without, begin to embarrass him, and the net of circumstances to entangle him, the fatal secret struggles, with still greater violence, to burst forth. It *must* be confessed—it *will* be confessed—there is no refuge from confession but suicide—and suicide is confession!   DANIEL WEBSTER.

HOW A MAN GETS UP IN THE MORNING.

Generally his wife tells him it is time to get up.

If she be in earnest, she emphasizes the assertion by a dig of her elbow in the direction of his ribs, and a flop which draws the blankets off his side of the bed onto her side.

He feels the cold air rush in, and knows something is the matter. He is still half asleep, and does not fully understand whether it is evening or morning. He wishes Eliza Ann would let him alone, and suffer him to go asleep; he doesn't want to be waked up in the middle of the night, and his head aching so badly. A man's head always aches when he does not want to be meddled with.

When at last he is brought to see that the sun is shining in at the window, he rises up a foot or so from the pillow, stares out of the window, yawns a half-dozen times, scratches his head vigorously, draws up his legs, stretches, grunts, says he is tired, and lies down again.

His wife comes to the rescue again, and by and by he manages to get up on his elbow, and look around the room as if he had never been there before. He has to form the acquaintance of all the furniture and fixtures over again. He looks at the pictures, and comments on the way that new chromo dangles over the fire-place. His wife hung it there herself, and she defends its right to dangle. He opposes, and argues to show he is right, and then he changes the subject, and wonders if the seven o'clock bell has struck. All this is to gain time—time to lie in bed a little longer.

After a while he puts out one foot, by way of a feeler. The cold air strikes it, and he draws it back, and his wife bounces up into a heap, and sharply tells him "she does wish he'd keep his icy feet away from her!" She shivers away to the marrow of her backbone. And as no loving husband who has sworn at the altar to love, cherish, and protect the woman of his bosom is justified in causing the marrow in her backbone to shiver, he withdraws that cold foot from her vicinity, and by the way of experiment puts the other foot out of bed.

Then he shivers, and cries "ugh!" and yawns again, and scratches the portion of his head which he did not hit before, and he stretches, and rubs his nose, and wonders what has become of his stockings. He left 'em right beside the bed the night before. He is positive about it. And as it is a well-known fact that a man always knows where he left his clothes when undressing, he finds one of his stockings in the wood-box, and the other on the bureau, under his wife's false hair and the dirty towel.

Nothing like order in this world; and if the average man is not orderly, then who is?

While he is getting into his pantaloons a button comes off. One always does. And it flies away to nowhere, and our man gets down on all fours, and looks under the bed, and up in the wall-basket, and into the water-pitcher, and all around for it, in vain.

"'Lizy Ann!" he exclaims; "I've lost off a button. I want it sewed on. I can't dress without it."

"Do wait till I get up!" says 'Lizy Ann, who is now deep in the mysteries of a new novel, which she has just taken from under her pillow, and is of course impatient at being disturbed. "A man is always in want!"

"Well, I've got to have this button sewed on," says he, tugging away at his suspenders.

And 'Lizy Ann reaches out and gets a needle and thread, and fishes up a button from her work-basket, and the sewing on of the button is an accomplished fact. And by the time that is done, it is discovered that a button is missing from his shirt. Nothing can be done until that button is fixed. Then his collar must be pinned down behind, so it won't "ride up."

Then he calls on 'Lizy Ann for a handkerchief. She tells him his handkerchiefs are right there in the second drawer.

He pulls the drawer out, away out, for a man can never do anything with a drawer unless it is away out, and he tumbles over the things it contains, and pitches out a shirt or two, and jams the drawer back with a stocking hanging over the edge, and a neck-tie caught in the back, and wonders what does make that drawer run so hard, and says there are no handkerchiefs there. And then he pulls out another drawer, and turns over a night-gown or two, and upsets a box of powder, and piles ribbons, and laces, and crimping-pins out on the floor, and gets his foot in his wife's work-basket, and unravels half a yard of that lovely edging she is knitting, and emphatically declares he wishes his things could be put where they belong.

Then 'Lizy Ann gets out of bed, and goes to his drawer and brings to view a pile of handkerchiefs which he has tumbled over, and gives it as her opinion that a man doesn't know anything.

Then he goes to the window and throws that open, and lets in the cold air, and tells 'Lizy Ann to hurry up and dress and the cold air won't hurt her, when she expostulates, and pleads cold feet and neuralgia.

And he slops the wall-paper in washing, and leaves hair in the comb, and gets hair oil on her best lace bow, and spatters his boot blacking over the carpet, and knocks the skin off his knuckles against the sink, and has to call on 'Lizy Ann for sticking plaster and arnica, and makes himself a nuisance generally; but he is a man, and was born with a man's carelessness within him, and she knows it, and would not have him changed into a woman for all the world.   KATE THORN.

SKETCH OF BONAPARTE.

Napoleon Bonaparte is fallen! We may now pause before that splendid prodigy, which towered among us like some ancient ruin, whose frown terrified the glance its magnificence attracted. Grand, gloomy, and peculiar, he sat upon the throne, a sceptered hermit, wrapt in the solitude of his own originality. A mind, bold, independent, and decisive—a will, despotic in its dictates—an energy that distanced expedition, and a conscience pliable to every touch of interest, marked the outline of this extraordinary character—the most extraordinary, perhaps, that, in the annals of this world, ever rose, or reigned, or fell.

Flung into life, in the midst of a revolution that quickened every energy of a people who acknowledge no superior, he commenced his course, a stranger by birth, and a scholar by charity! With no friend but his sword, and no fortune, but his talents, he rushed in the list where rank, and wealth, and genius had arrayed themselves, and competition fled from him as from the glance of destiny. He knew no motive but interest—he acknowledged no criterion but success—he worshiped no God but ambition, and, with an eastern devotion, he knelt at the shrine of his idolatry.

Subsidiary to this, there was no creed that he did not profess, there was no opinion that he did not promulgate; in the hope of a dynasty, he upheld the Crescent; for the sake of a divorce, he bowed before the Cross; the orphan of St. Louis, he became the adopted child of the Republic; and, with a parricidal ingratitude, on the ruins both of the throne and tribune, he reared the throne of his despotism. A professed Catholic, he imprisoned the Pope; a pretended patriot, he impoverished the country; and, in the name of Brutus, he grasped without remorse, and wore without shame, the diadem of the Cæsars! Through this pantomime of policy, fortune played the clown to his caprices. At his touch, crowns crumbled, beggars reigned, systems vanished, the wildest theories took the color of his whim, and all that was venerable, and all that was novel, changed places with the rapidity of a drama.

Even apparent defeat assumed the appearance of victory —his flight from Egypt confirmed his destiny—ruin itself only elevated him to empire. But, if his fortune was great, his genius was transcendent; decision flashed upon his counsels; and it was the same to decide and to perform. To inferior intellects his combinations appeared perfectly impossible, his plans perfectly impracticable; but, in his hands, simplicity marked their development, and success vindicated their adoption. His person partook the char-

acter of his mind—if the one never yielded in the cabinet,
the other never bent in the field.   Nature had no obstacle
that he did not surmount—space no opposition that he did
not spurn; and whether amid Alpine rocks, Arabian sands,
or Polar snows, he seemed proof against peril, and em-
powered with ubiquity!

   The whole continent trembled at beholding the audacity
of his designs, and the miracle of their execution. Skepti-
cism bowed to the prodigies of his performance; romance
assumed the air of history; nor was there aught too incred-
ible for belief, or too fanciful for expectation, when the
world saw a subaltern of Corsica waving his imperial flag
over her most ancient capitals. All the visions of antiquity
became commonplaces in his contemplation; kings were
his people—nations were his outposts; and he disposed of
courts, and crowns, and camps, and churches, and cabi-
nets, as if they were titular dignitaries of the chess-board!
Amid all these changes, he stood immutable as adamant.

   It mattered little whether in the field or in the drawing-
room—with the mob or the levee—wearing the Jacobin
bonnet or the iron crown—banishing a Braganza, or es-
pousing a Hapsburg—dictating peace on a raft to the Czar
of Russia, or contemplating defeat at the gallows of Leip-
sic—he was still the same military despot!

   In this wonderful combination, his affectations of literature must not be omitted. The jailer of the press, he affected the patronage of letters—the proscriber of books,
he encouraged philosophy—the persecutor of authors and
the murderer of printers, he yet pretended to be the protec-
tor of learning! Such a medley of contradictions, and,
at the same time, such an individual consistency, were
never united in the same character. A royalist,—a repub-
lican, and an emperor—a Mohammedan—a Catholic and a
patron of the synagogue—a subaltern and a sovereign—a
traitor and a tyrant—a Christian and an infidel—he was,
through all his vicissitudes, the same stern, impatient, in-

flexible original—the same mysterious, incomprehensible self—the man without a model, and without a shadow.

CHARLES PHILLIPS.

THE LATE MR. McGLUCKEN.

"Mr. Peters," said the editor to the new reporter, "you say you were personally acquainted with the deceased, Mr. McGlucken?"

"Yes, sir."

"And you are certain of the facts that you have given in his obituary notice?"

"Well, tolerably certain."

"Because in describing his appearance you say that he had a Roman nose, and only one eye, and that there was a wart upon it. Do I understand you that the wart was upon the Roman nose or the eye?" The expression is not perfectly clear.

"The nose, of course."

"You remark, also, that Mr. McGlucken's nose was badly injured in the railroad accident at Newark in consequence of the bridge giving way. Now, I don't catch the drift of this. Do you mean that the railroad accident resulted from the breaking of the bridge of Mr. McGlucken's nose, or that the bridge of his nose gave way after the accident, or that the nose was hurt by the railroad bridge giving way, or how? You are not definite enough."

"I refer to the railroad bridge."

"Ah! Then you go on to say that Mr. McGlucken married in 1862, but that after a year of too brief happiness his wife died suddenly, leaving him with eight dear little children, the eldest of whom was but seven years of age. This is calculated to fill the minds of readers with perplexity. Are you sure there were *eight* children? And if so, that the oldest was but seven years of age?"

"I forgot to state that Mrs. McGlucken had been married before, and that there were three sets of twins."

"The omission is important. I notice that you say, in the fourth paragraph from the bottom, that McGlucken went to sea when he was a young man, and that his craft was stove at the Feejee Islands. Then immediately afterward you remark that at poker he never had a rival. Now, I can hardly believe you mean it, and yet do you know that a superficial reader, glancing over your article, might easily get the impression that McGlucken went to sea in a stove, and somehow or other, managed to row himself ashore on the Feejee Islands with a poker. Read it over and see for yourself. I tell you, Mr. Peters, this kind of a want of definiteness won't do for a newspaper. It confuses people's minds, and maddens them, and brings them down here with murder in their hearts."

"I admit that it is not exactly clear."

"But this is not the worst. What do you mean when you say, in the fifth paragraph, that while Mr. McGlucken lived in Perkiomen township, he was somewhat lame for a few years, and that he had the largest corn in the country —it was more than eight feet high? Now, do you mean that he had a corn eight feet high, or that he had corn in his field eight feet high, and if the latter, why do you associate the corn with Mr. McGlucken's lameness? Don't you see for yourself that most persons would get the notion that McGlucken's lameness was caused by a corn which grew up through his boot and was fastened to his hat? Why, Mr. Peters, if we were to print a thing like that I believe this office would be gutted by a mob before night."

"I see; I must rewrite that."

"Right afterward, next to that singular reference to the fact that his aunt persisted in putting on her gum shoes whenever she went to bed, and that his grandmother swallowed her spectacles three times in church, you remark that 'in 1874 Mr. McGlucken was taken with torpidity of the liver, whereupon he joined the Swedenborgian church and voted the Greenback ticket regularly.' You see you fail to make the thing connect. People will want to know *how* torpidity of the liver drove him over to the Swedenborgians, and why a Swedenborgian with an ineffective liver should have a propensity to support the Greenbackers. And no sooner does the bewildered reader give up the problem than you add, respecting Mr. McGlucken's connection with the church choir, that 'he was a fine singer generally, but on this particular Sunday he rode his favorite horse to church, and, as he had the heaves, he had to stop before reaching his destination, so he missed his usual participation in the services,' &c., &c. I pledge you my word of honor, Mr. Peters, as a man who has his finger on the public pulse, that there will be a million people around here to-morrow perfectly savage to know whether McGlucken had the heaves, or whether the horse had! No, Mr. Peters, it won't do! It really won't. I want to put in a good obituary of McGlucken. I know you want to do him justice. I can see your sympathetic feeling running all through this article. It is chock-full of genuine emotion. You really mourn for McGlucken. But hang it, young man, if I should let the billowy tumults of sorrow that rage in your soul boil out into the columns of the *Daily Argus* in this particular form, I should have the whole McGlucken family after me with a libel suit, and within forty-eight hours all the insane asylums in the State would be so crowded that the patients couldn't breathe! No, you must overhaul it; furbish it up; rewrite it; remodel it; lick it into shape. I'll give you one more chance."

Mr. Peters handed in his resignation, and sought a position as conductor of a horse-car. MAX ADELER.

A SONG OF THE CANTEEN.

There are bonds of all sorts in this world of ours,
Fetters of friendship and ties of flowers,
    And true lovers' knots, I ween;
The girl and the boy are bound by a kiss,
But there's never a bond, old friend, like this—.
    We have drank from the same canteen.

It was sometimes water and sometimes milk,
And sometimes applejack, fine as silk,
    But whate'er the tipple has been,
We shared it together in bane or bliss,
And I warm to you, friend, when I think of this—
    We have drank from the same canteen.

The rich and the great sit down to dine,
And they quaff each other in sparkling wine,
    From glasses of crystal and green;
But I guess in their golden potations they miss
The warmth of regard to be found in this—
    We have drank from the same canteen.

We shared our blankets and tents together,
And have fought and marched in all kinds of
      weather,
    And hungry and full have we been;
Had days of battle and days of rest,
But this memory I cling to and love the best—
    We have drank from the same canteen.

For when wounded I lay on the outer slope,
With my blood flowing fast, and but little hope
    Upon which my faint spirit could lean,
Oh, then, I remember, you crawled to my side,
And bleeding so fast it seemed both must have
      died,
    We drank from the same canteen.
            CHARLES G. HALPINE.

MRS. GRUBBS' RAILROAD CLAIM.

Mrs. Grubbs (excitedly)—Do you mean to say you don't intend to make a claim on the railroad company for my damaged trunk? You know it was a beautiful new trunk, and it's absolutely ruined, and the contents are hardly recognizable.

Mr. Grubbs (wise in his generation)—It is very unfortunate, my dear; but never mind, I'll get you a new trunk, and——

Mrs. Grubbs—Indeed you won't. If you are not man enough to demand your rights, I'll do it myself, so there!

Mrs. Grubbs (in railroad office building an hour later)— I wish to see the person in charge of the damaged baggage department.

Door-tender—Never heard of any sich department, mum.

Mrs. Grubbs—Well, I took passage over this road a few days ago, and when my trunk was delivered it was almost demolished and half the contents——

Door-tender—Yes, mum—very busy now, mum; can't stop to chat about family affairs, mum.

Mrs. Grubbs—Huh! Where is the president's office?

Door-tender—Right there, mum.

Mrs. Grubbs (after half an hour's vain knocking at the door)—I can't make any one hear.

Door-tender—No, mum; the president is on a trip to Chiny fer his health, but that's his office, mum.

Mrs. Grubbs—Will you be kind enough to tell me who comes next to the president?

Door-tender—First vice-president, mum.

Mrs. Grubbs—Where is his office?

Door-tender—With the president, mum.

Mrs. Grubbs—But that office is closed.

Door-tender—Yes, mum; he's in Chicago, but he'll be back next week.

Mrs. Grubbs—I'd like to know who's in charge here.

Door-tender—I am, mum.

Mrs. Grubbs (impatiently)—Who is in charge of the building?

Door-tender—Mr. Feelbig, mum.

Mrs. Grubbs—Where is he?

Door-tender—Down stairs, bossin' the coons what's siftin' ashes, mum.

Mrs. Grubbs—Humph! What is his position?

Door-tender—Head janitor, mum.

Mrs. Grubbs (with an inspiration)—Is the superintendent in?

Door-tender—Don't know, mum, as we've got any superintendent, mum. You see, Mr. Feelbig used to be called the superintendent of the building, but——

Mrs. Grubbs (with a great effort at self-control)—I mean the superintendent of the railroad.

Door-tender—Oh! Why didn't ye say so? I don't know whether he be in or not, fer he's mostly on the road, but his office is on the fifth floor, mum.

Mrs. Grubbs (to elevator boy)—I wish to go to the fifth floor.

Elevator Boy—Nothin' there, ma'am, but offices.

Mrs. Grubbs—I know it.

Elevator Boy— Oh! Who de ye want ter see?

Mrs. Grubbs—The superintendent.

Elevator Boy (picking up a dime novel, and settling himself in one corner)—He ain't in.

Mrs. Grubbs—Then I want to see the next one in charge.

Elevator Boy—Who?

Mrs. Grubbs—I don't know; whoever is in charge at this time.

Elevator Boy—I don't know who is in charge, either,

but I'll take ye up, only ye mustn't stay too long chinning to the clerks. It ain't allowed. Here ye are. Fifth floor, mum.

Mrs. Grubbs (entering nearest door and addressing the first person in view)—I wish to see about a trunk——

First Clerk—Baggage-room —other side river, madam.

Mrs. Grubbs—About a trunk which was badly damaged——

First Clerk—Nex' desk.

Mrs. Grubbs (with a sigh of infinite relief) I called in regard to a damaged trunk——.

Second Clerk—Nex' desk.

Mrs. Grubbs—My trunk was badly damaged—in fact, ruined——

Third (and last) Clerk—Nex' room.

Mrs. Grubbs (in next room)—The baggage handlers of your road——

Official (starting up)—My gracious! On strike?

Mrs. Grubbs (with spirit)—They struck my trunk against a stone wall or something, and nearly demolished it.

Official (resuming his seat)—Nex' floor.

Mrs. Grubbs—Which floor?

Official—Nexisaid.

Mrs. Grubbs—Up or down?

Official—Um—down.

Mrs. Grubbs (to the elevator boy)—Fourth floor, please.

Elevator Boy—Sell anything?

Mrs. Grubbs—I am not a peddler. I wish to go to the fourth floor.

Elevator Boy (with a startled air)—Ye ain't a relation of any of the vice-presidents, are ye?

Mrs. Grubbs (shortly)—No.

Elevator Boy (with restored equilibrium)—I thought ye couldn't be, from y'r clothes. This floor is full o' vice-presidents. Fourth, madam.

Mrs. Grubbs (catching sight of a benevolent-looking personage just leaving an office)—I beg your pardon, sir, but I want some one to—to—I want to see some one about a damaged trunk, very badly damaged—in fact, ruined.

Benevolent Party (reflectively)—It might be well to see the ninth assistant vice-president's seventeenth assistant secretary, room 93, tenth floor.

Mrs. Grubbs—Oh, thank you! I began to think I never would find the right office.

Benevolent Party—Take the elevator to the right, madam. I am very glad to be of service. Good-day, madam.

Mrs. Grubbs—Tenth floor, please.

Elevator Boy—Yes'm. You must be sellin' something, ain't you? I won't tell, 'deed and double, but I think ye might give me a little if it's good to eat.

Mrs. Grubbs—This is simply a roll of music, and a few other things I got as I came along, thinking I'd be through here in a few minutes.

Elevator Boy—Oh, I forgot to tell ye. The elevator don't run above the seventh floor to-day—making some repairs up there.

Mrs. Grubbs—Dear me! How do the clerks get up?

Elevator Boy—I let 'em off here an' they go up the fire-escape. Want to see any one in partic'lar?

Mrs. Grubbs—Yes, the—the—well, it's one of the assistant secretaries.

Elevator Boy—Here comes one now.

Mrs. Grubbs (stepping into the hall)—I wish to see the —the tenth assistant president's ninth assistant——

Assistant Secretary—No such person exists, madam.

Mrs. Grubbs—Hasn't he a ninth assistant sec——

Assistant Secretary (impressively)—There is no tenth assistant president, madam.

Mrs. Grubbs—Let me see. Oh! It was a vice-president.

Assistant Secretary (impatiently)—Well?

Mrs. Grubbs—Well, I want to see the ninth assistant pres—I mean vice-president's——.

Assistant Secretary—He is not in.

Mrs. Grubbs—Not the vice-president himself, but——

Assistant Secretary—I understand. The ninth assistant vice-president. He is not in.

Mrs. Grubbs—I don't want to see him. I want to see his ninth—oh, now I remember—I want to see the ninth assistant vice-president's seventeenth assistant secretary.

Assistant Secretary—I am he, madam. What can I do for you?

Mrs. Grubbs—It's about a damaged trunk—

Assistant Secretary—Great snakes! Trunks are not in my department. Pardon me, but I'm in a great hurry.

Mrs. Grubbs—Wait just one moment. A gentleman whom I met coming from an office down stairs referred me to you. I'm sure he is the president, or something.

Assistant Secretary—President's away, ditto superintendent. What kind of a looking gentleman was he?

Mrs. Grubbs—Oh, real benevolent looking, and he took so much interest in my case, and——

Assistant Secretary—Guess he doesn't belong here. Big or little man?

Mrs. Grubbs—A tall, handsome, portly old gentleman, with white side-whiskers, and I remember he wore a remarkable antique ring, Egyptian design.

Assistant Secretary—Oh! Now I know who you mean. He's a distant relative of the ninth assistant vice; and now I think of it, a friend of his once lost a lot of cattle in a blizzard while in transit, and to oblige him the ninth assistant vice got me to fix the matter up somehow and send him a check for part of the losses; but that was freight, you know, *through freight;* it wasn't baggage. I have nothing to do with baggage—hope I never will have either.

Mrs. Grubbs—But where shall I go?

Assistant Secretary—Oh, nearly all the hotels in this city are good—mere matter of——

Mrs. Grubbs—I mean to whom shall I apply about my trunk?

Assistant Secretary—I'm sure I don't know; you ought to have thought of that before you came here. I must hurry, madam.

Mrs. Grubbs—(groping wearily along the halls)—I wish to see——

First Passer—Next floor.

Mrs. Grubbs—Is the official who has charge of the baggage which——

Second Passer—Over t' depot. Don't b'long here.

Mrs. Grubbs (desperately, to another)—When this railroad company sells tickets——

Third Passer—Yes, indeed, madam; but we don't sell tickets in this building. Ticket office down street. Here, boy! Hold that elevator a moment. Lady wants t' go down. Good-day, madam. Most luxurious traveling in the country, as you'll soon find.

Mrs. Grubb (to elevator boy while dropping down)—Isn't there any head to this establishment?

Elevator Boy—Ain't much else but head, I guess. You ain't been on the second floor yet. Want to get off? I won't tell.

Mrs. Grubbs (humbly)—Ye-e-s.

Elevator Boy—Tackle them fellers there. They bought five books of a lady yestiday, but she were younger 'n you.

Mrs. Grubbs (entering first office, and determined that her errand sha'n't be misunderstood)—My trunk was completely ruined on this road, and I want to see the proper official about it.

First Clerk—Nex' room.

Mrs. Grubbs (entering next room)—I am determined to find the official who has charge of the—the baggage dep——

First Clerk—Bag'm'ster over depot. Here, boy! Show lady cross-town cars.

Mrs. Grubbs (at depot an hour later)—My trunk was utterly ruined on this road, and——

Depot Master—Lost?

Mrs. Grubbs—No, smashed; smashed all to pieces.

Depot Master—Old trunk, I s'pose?

Mrs. Grubbs (with some asperity)—A brand-new one.

Depot Master—Well, people as buys these 'ere cheap paper trunks jest 'cause——

Mrs. Grubbs (vehemently)—My trunk was thick leather, bound with iron.

Depot Master—Ye might a known better 'n to buy a heavy thing like that, as would break of its own weight. Now here is a trunk what ain't hard to lift, and——

Mrs. Grubbs—My trunk was damaged and I want pay for it.

Depot Master—Over t' gen'l office.

Mrs. Grubbs (out of all patience)—But I just came from the general office——

Depot Master—Well, ye needn't scowl at me 'bout it. I didn't bring ye. If a man 'ud put on half the airs wot you do I'd knock 'im down. We ain't got no money here ter start benevolent societies fer people with lost trunks. The general office is where the money is, can't ye see that? Take the cross-town cars.

Mrs. Grubbs (an hour later, at general office)—Are you connected with this company, sir?

Pompous Individual—Only in an advisory capacity. I am one of its attorneys.

Mrs. Grubbs—Oh. Well I have a claim for damages for a——

Pompous Individual—I'll see your lawyer at any time, madam, but, remember, if you want to sue, we've got the best lawyers in the State, and we own two-thirds of the legislature and half the judges. Better drop it. Good-day, madam.

Mrs. Grubbs (after two hours further and equally fruitless questioning)—Can you direct me——

Policeman—Yis, mum, Oi can direct ye to the door, an' that's phat I come for. It's complained t' me that ye've been hangin' an' loafin' about the buildin' all day wid no apparent means o' respectable support, an' it's out ye'll be goin' av y'r own accord or Oi'll put yez out. Move on, now.

Mrs. Grubbs (entering her own home, just before dark) —Mercy! I feel as if I should faint. How long have you been home, my dear?

Mr. Grubbs—Only about an hour. Well, did you settle about the trunk?

Mrs. Grubbs—Yes. Just before reaching the house I happened to see a drayman who once did some work for us. I immediately hired him to come get the trunk and dump it into the East River.   CHARLES W. FOSTER.

IMPORTANCE OF THE UNION.

I profess, sir, in my career hitherto to have kept steadily in view the prosperity and honor of the whole country, and the preservation of our federal Union. It is to that Union we owe our safety at home, and our consideration and dignity abroad. It is to that Union we are chiefly indebted for whatever makes us most proud of our country. That Union we reached only by the discipline of our virtues, in the severe school of adversity. It had its origin

in the necessities of disordered finance, prostrate com-
merce, and ruined credit.

Under its benign influences, these great interests immediately awoke, as from the dead, and sprang forth with
newness of life.   Every year of its duration has teemed
with fresh proofs of its utility and its blessings; and, although our territory has stretched out wider and wider,
and our population spread farther and farther, they have
not outrun its protection or its benefits.   It has been to
us all a copious fountain of national, social, and personal
happiness.

I have not allowed myself, sir, to look beyond the Union,
to see what might lie hidden in the dark recess behind.   I
have not coolly weighed the chances of preserving liberty,
when the bonds that unite us together shall be broken
asunder.   I have not accustomed myself to hang over the
precipice of disunion to see whether, with my short sight,
I can fathom the depth of the abyss below; nor could I
regard him as a safe counselor in the affairs of this government, whose thoughts should be mainly bent on consider-
ing, not how the Union should be best preserved, but how
tolerable might be the condition of the people, when it
shall be broken up and destroyed.

While the Union lasts. we have high, exciting, gratifying
prospects spread out before us, for us and our children.
Beyond that I seek not to penetrate the vail.   God grant
that, in my day, at least, that curtain may not rise.   God
grant that on my vision never may be opened what lies
behind.   When my eyes shall be turned to behold, for the
last time, the sun in heaven, may I not see him shining
on the broken and dishonored fragments of a once glorious Union; on States dissevered, discordant, belligerent,
on a land rent with civil feuds, or drenched, it may be, in
fraternal blood!

Let their last feeble and lingering glance rather behold
the gorgeous ensign of the republic, now known and hon-

ored throughout the earth, still full high advanced, its arms and trophies streaming in their original luster, not a stripe erased or polluted, nor a single star obscured— bearing for its motto no such miserable interrogatory as— what is all this worth? Nor those other words of delusion and folly—Liberty first, and Union afterward—but everywhere, spread all over in characters of living light, blazing on all its ample folds as they float under the sea and over the land, and in every wind over the whole heavens, that other sentiment dear to every true American heart—Liberty *and* Union, NOW AND FOREVER, ONE AND INSEPARABLE!

DANIEL WEBSTER.

THE AMERICAN FLAG.

When Freedom, from her mountain height,
  Unfurled her standard to the air,
She tore the azure robe of night,
  And set the stars of glory there.
She mingled with its gorgeous dyes
The milky baldric of the skies,
And striped its pure, celestial white,
With streakings of the morning light;
Then, from his mansion in the sun,
She called her eagle bearer down,
And gave into his mighty hand
The symbol of her chosen land.

Majestic monarch of the cloud,
  Who rear'st aloft thy regal form,
To hear the tempest trumpings loud
And see the lightning lances driven,
  When strive the warriors of the storm,
And rolls the thunder-drum of heaven,
Child of the sun! to thee 'tis given

To guard the banner of the free,
To hover in the sulphur smoke,
To ward away the battle-stroke,
And bid its blendings shine afar,
Like rainbows on the cloud of war,
    The harbingers of victory!

Flag of the brave! thy folds shall fly,
    The sign of hope and triumph high,
When speaks the signal trumpet tone,
    And the long line comes gleaming on.
Ere yet the life-blood, warm and wet,
    Has dimmed the glistening bayonet,
Each soldier eye shall brightly turn
    To where thy sky-born glories burn;
And, as his springing steps advance,
Catch war and vengeance from the glance.
And when the cannon-mouthings loud
    Heave in wild wreaths the battle-shroud,
And gory sabers rise and fall
Like shoots of flame on midnight's pall;
    Then shall thy meteor glances glow,
And cowering foes shall sink beneath
    Each gallant arm, that strikes below
That lovely messenger of death.

Flag of the seas! on ocean wave
    Thy stars shall glitter o'er the brave;
When death, careering on the gale,
    Sweeps darkly round the bellied sail,
And frightened waves rush wildly back
    Before the broadside's reeling rack,
Each dying wanderer of the sea
    Shall look at once to heaven and thee,
And smile to see thy splendors fly
In triumph o'er his closing eye.

Flag of the free heart's hope and home!
   By angel hands to valor given;
Thy stars have lit the welkin dome,
   And all thy hues were born in heaven.
Forever float that standard sheet!
   Where breathes the foe but falls before us,
With Freedom's soil beneath our feet,
   And Freedom's banner streaming o'er us?
              JOSEPH RODMAN DRAKE.

THE LITTLE SISTER OF CHARITY.

Young Harry Gilflory was just twenty-four,
And had to his credit a million or more;
To him the great world was a garden of flowers,
And he, like a butterfly, wasted his hours.
He frequented clubs, and he drove his fast horse—
Was the pet of the belles, and their mammas, of course;
He had nothing to do but kill time, and I fear
This cost him at least twenty thousand a year.

Like many possessors of very great wealth,
He thought more of pleasures that kill than of health;
The wine-cup he'd quaff till his wits went astray,
And sometimes he'd cling to it day after day,
Till nature gave out, and he'd wake at the close
Of a lengthened debauch, sick, unnerved, and morose—
A prey to remorse, and disgusted to think
Of the follies he'd wrought while demented by drink.

'Twas after a turn of this kind that young Gil—
Dejected, unnerved by excess, and quite ill—
Lounged in his hotel, to all outward things blind,
At war with himself and with all of his kind;
His young features wore an expression forlorn,

His clothes were bedaubed, and in some places torn,
His hair was unkempt, and his eyes were blood-shot,
And he looked very much like a penniless sot.

Though society's pet, and by every one known,
Not one spoke to Gil as he sat there alone;
He was left unmolested amid the rude din,
Till a small beggar-girl from the street ventured in;
Her clothing was thin, and her features were pinched,
But from the rude gazers the child never flinched;
She must have been less than a dozen years old,
But a long fight with hardship had rendered her bold.

To each lounger the little petitioner went—
"Please give me a copper, sir—only a cent!
Since morning I've had not a morsel to eat,
And I'm tired, *so* tired, from walking the street!"
Some gave her a penny, some pushed her aside;
But, firm and undaunted, she every one tried,
Till she came to our hero, the wretched Gilflory,
Held out her wee hand, and repeated her story.

"You've had nothing to eat since the morning, you say?"
Gil sullenly growled. "Little girl go away!
For three days *I've* tasted no food; so you see,
You're far better off, you young beggar, than me!"
The girl hung her head and had nothing to say,
But she heaved a deep sigh, and walked slowly away;
She paused at the door, hesitated, and then
Turned quickly, and faced young Gilflory again.

"Poor man!" she exclaimed; I'm *so* sorry for you!"
And her pitying eyes filled with heavenly dew,
And her voice had a pathos as tender and sweet
As our Saviour's when Magdalen knelt at his feet.
"Three days without eating! Oh, that is *too* bad!
Here, take these five cents, and you'll make me so glad.

You know you can't live without something to eat,
And I can get help from some one on the street."

From his indolent stupor Gilflory awoke,
At first he felt sure that the child meant to joke;
He looked at her keenly, but naught could he trace
Save angelic sympathy in her young face.
"By Heaven! *she means it!* ' he cried, in surprise;
"Her young bosom heaves; there are tears in her eyes;
Both language and accent speak pity and love—
She offers *me* money, and means it, by Jove!

"This poor little waif is a princess to-night,
And I am the subject that pales in her light.
She has taught me a lesson that cannot depart,
While reason remains and there's warmth in my heart;
She has taught me the lesson that Christ taught of old—
That the heart which can *feel* is the genuine gold,
And that in His bright home most blessed He'll call
Not those who gave largely, but those who gave *all*.

"Come here, thou frail waif of small form but big heart,
Gilflory's the beggar—the lady thou art!"
And quietly taking his hat from his head,
He passed it around to each person, and said:
"I want five dollars, please, not a single cent less,
For this angel of light in a calico dress!"

They gave without grumbling; but then, don't you see,
They gave to a young millionaire on a spree,
Who passed it in turn to the "angel of light
In the calico dress," and kept sober that night.

FRANCIS S. SMITH.

THE WAR IN AMERICA.

My lords: I cannot concur in a blind and servile address, which approves, and endeavors to sanctify the monstrous measures which have heaped disgrace and misfortune upon us. This, my lords, is a perilous and tremendous moment! It is not a time for adulation. The smoothness of flattery can not now avail—cannot save us in this rugged and awful crisis. It is now necessary to instruct the throne in the language of truth. We must dispel the illusion and the darkness which envelop it, and display, in its full danger and-true colors, the ruin that is brought to our doors.

Can the minister of the day now presume to expect a continuance of support in this ruinous infatuation? Can parliament be so dead to its dignity and its duty as to be thus deluded into the loss of the one and the violation of the other? To give an unlimited credit and support for the steady perseverance in measures not proposed for our parliamentary advice, but dictated and forced upon us— in measures, I say, my lords, which have reduced this late flourishing empire to ruin and contempt! "But yesterday, and England might have stood against the world; now none so poor to do her reverence." I use the words of a poet; but, though it be poetry, it is no fiction.

My lords, this ruinous and ignominious situation, where we cannot act with success, nor suffer with honor, calls upon us to remonstrate in the strongest and loudest language of truth, to rescue the ear of majesty from the delusions which surround it. The desperate state of our arms abroad is in part known. No man thinks more highly of them than I do. I love and honor the English troops. I know their virtues and their valor. I know they can achieve anything except impossibilities; and I know that the conquest of English America *is an impossibility.* You cannot, I venture to say it, *you cannot conquer America!*

You may swell every expense and every effort still more extravagantly; pile and accumulate every assistance you can buy or borrow; traffic and barter with every little, pitiful German prince that sells and sends his subjects to the shambles of a foreign prince; your efforts are forever vain and impotent—doubly so from this mercenary aid on which you rely; for it irritates, to an incurable resentment, the minds of your enemies, to over run them with the mercenary sons of rapine and plunder, devoting them and their possessions to the rapacity of hireling cruelty! If I were an American, as I am an Englishman, while a foreign troop was landed in my country, I *never* would lay down my arms—*never—never—never!*

But, my lords, who is the man that, in addition to these disgraces and mischiefs of our army, has dared to authorize and associate to our arms the tomahawk and scalping-knife of the savage? to call into civilized alliance the wild and inhuman savage of the woods; to delegate to the merciless Indian the defense of disputed rights, and to wage the horrors of his barbarous war against our brethren? My lords, these enormities cry aloud for redress and punishment. Unless thoroughly done away, it will be a stain on the national character. It is a violation of the Constitution.

Infected with the mercenary spirit of robbery and rapine; familiarized to the horrid scenes of savage cruelty, it can no longer boast of the noble and generous principles which dignify a soldier; no longer sympathize with the dignity of the royal banner; nor feel the pride, pomp, and circumstance of glorious war, "that make ambition virtue!" What makes ambition virtue? The sense of *honor!*

But is the sense of honor consistent with a spirit of plunder, or the practice of murder? Can it flow from mercenary motives, or can it prompt to cruel deeds? Besides these murderers and plunderers, let me ask our ministers—what other allies have they acquired? What *other powers* have they associated to their cause? Have they entered into alliance with the *king of the gipsies?* Nothing, my lords, is too low or two ludicrous to be consistent with their counsels.

I am astonished, shocked, to hear such principles confessed—to hear them avowed in this House, or in this country; principles equally unconstitutional, inhuman, and unchristian! My lords, we are called upon, as members of this House, as men, as Christian men, to protest against such notions standing near the throne, polluting the ear of majesty.

"*That God and nature put into our hands?*" I know not what ideas that lord may entertain of God and nature, but I know that such abominable principles are equally abhorrent to religion and humanity. What! to attribute the sacred sanction of God and nature to the massacres of the Indian scalping-knife—to the cannibal savage torturing, murdering, roasting, and eating—literally, my lords, *eating* the mangled victims of his barbarous battles! Such horrible notions shock every precept of religion, divine or natural, and every generous feeling of humanity.

These abominable principles, and this more abominable avowal of them, demand the most decisive indignation. I call upon that right reverend bench, those holy ministers of the gospel, and pious pastors of our church—I conjure them to join in the holy work, and vindicate the religion of their God. I appeal to the wisdom and the law of that learned bench, to defend and support the justice of their country.

I call upon the bishops, to interpose the unsullied sanctity of their lawn; upon the learned judges, to interpose the purity of their ermine, to save us from this pollution. I call upon the honor of your lordships, to reverence the dignity of your ancestors, and to maintain your own. I call upon the spirit and humanity of my country, to vindicate the national character. I invoke the genius of the Constitution. From the tapestry that adorns these walls, the immortal ancestor of this noble lord frowns with indignation at the disgrace of his country.

EARL OF CHATHAM.

WHAT THE SKIPPER SAID.

We were all sailing down along the Jersey coast in a yacht, and the greenhorns in the party were bothering the skipper with questions. We sighted a light-house, and Mr. Anderson, who hailed from Ohio, and had never seen one before, asked what *that* was.

"That," said the skipper, rather scornfully, "is a light— a flash-light."

"What makes it flash?" inquired Mr. Anderson.

"Don't you know what makes it flash?" asked the skipper.

"No; what?"

"Well, you know what a lightning-bug is, don't you? The government has a place for breeding them, over here at Egg Harbor. They've crossed them and crossed them, using the selected varieties every time, until now they turn out a lightning-bug as big as a goose, and bigger. I've seen 'em weigh from eighty to ninety pounds, and carrying an illuminated end that would make a locomotive head-light look like darkness—actually look as black as ink."

"How do they raise them?"

"Feed 'em on musquitoes. A healthy bug'll eat half a bushel of New Jersey musquitoes at a meal. Government employs boys to catch the musquitoes in traps in the swamps. They keep the lightning-bugs in iron cages on account of the heat. You put fifteen or twenty of 'em together and get 'em excited, and they'll make it so hot in the cage in the coldest day in winter, that the keepers have to put ice around the cages to prevent them from melting."

"How about the light-houses?"

"When the government wants to 'start a light-house, they make a requisition for a bug, and he is carried off in a cage with a boy to stand behind and fan his fire-works so's to keep 'em cool. Then they put him on top of a light-house, and set him at work. If he doesn't flash his light often enough, the man tickles him under the wing with a hoe-handle, or something, and when he persists in working in the day-time, the keeper has to mesmerize him to prevent him from undermining his constitution."

"Wonderful!" said Mr. Anderson.

"I had no idea of such a thing," said Mr. O'Brien.

The skipper seemed encouraged to go on, and try to do so a little better.

"Yes," he said, "the whole thing is very curious. Now you wouldn't believe how long that light-house over there is?"

"How long is it?"

"Well, about eight or nine hundred yards. Possibly longer."

"No?"

"Yes. You see they began to build it in 1809. But the foundation was soft over on the beach there, and so the structure gradually sunk away. In about two years the lantern was only six feet above the ground. They had to build right on top of it, and as that made it heavier, of course it sank farther. One night the keeper accidentally overslept himself, and when he woke up the lantern was beneath the surface of the sand. It took nearly a whole day to dig him out. And so, you know, the government went on adding to the light-house year after year, and the building kept on sinking, until now you can go down stairs in that light-house well on to a mile toward the cen-

ter of the earth. The inspector told me they would con-
tinue to build, just to see where it would go to. The
board, I understand, rather expects ultimately to strike
China, and to bring about an arrangement for having the
whole of our tea trade with that country done up and down
the stairs of that light-house. Be rough on the Pacific
railroads, won't it?"

"Most extraordinary thing I ever heard of!" exclaimed
Mr. Anderson.

"I can hardly believe it," said Mr. O'Brien.

"I don t ask you to believe it," said the skipper. "I'm
only giving you the facts, and you can do what you please
with them. Now, there's the Barnegat light; that was not
built for a light-house. It was put there by a convulsion
of nature."

"How?"

"Why, there was a man lived on that spot named William McGuigan, and he wanted to sink a well. He had to
go two hundred and thirty seven feet before he struck
water; then he bricked the well in, and was satisfied. One
night, thirteen months later, there was an earthquake
along the coast here, and many supposed it was caused by
volcanic action, for in the morning, when McGuigan went
out to get a pitcher of water for breakfast, he found that
his well had been shot up out of the ground, and was
standing at that very minute two hundred and twenty-six
feet above the surface of his back yard. Subsequently he
went to Indiana to live with his wife's mother, and he sold
the well out to the Light-house Board, who put a stair-
case and a couple of boys in it, and to-day it's the finest
light on the Jersey coast."

"It is queer," said Mr. Anderson, "that no notice of so
remarkable an occurrence should have appeared in the
papers."

"The papers!" exclaimed the skipper, contemptuously.
"It's mighty little they know about what goes on down

here! Did you ever see in any of them any account of the death of Thomas Shanahan, the keeper of the Absecom light, a few years ago? Well, sir, one night, while Shanahan was in the lantern, four flights of stairs fell away from the top, and Shanahan was very much worried how to get down. When morning came he got desperate. He took the lightning-bug out of the lantern, straddled himself on its back, and stuck his penknife into it to make it fly.''

"Did he get down safely?"

"He got down, but one leg accidentally rested against the hot end of the bug, and when he reached the ground his leg was burned to a crisp, and he died in two hours. The bug flew over into the pines in Atlantic County, and set fire to eight hundred thousand dollars' worth of timber."

"Awful!" ejaculated Mr. Anderson.

"Those keepers have a hard time, any way," said the skipper, as he jammed his helm hard-aport. "I know one of 'em, over here at Long Branch, that is ruined for life --absolutely ruined."

"How?"

"Why, he's been going up and down those light-house stairs for twenty-two years, four times a day, and sticking close to work, taking no other exercise. What's the consequence? Consequence is that he can't walk straight to save his life! Forgotten how. He'll make fifteen or twenty circles in going across the street, and on Sundays he has to start one hour ahead of his wife, because he has so much farther to go; and even then, very often, church is half over and the collection taken up before he gets into his pew. I've known that man to walk eleven miles in going a distance of three-quarters of a mile, and the queer thing about it is that when he stands perfectly still it makes his head swim. Even his bedstead is swung on a pivot and revolved by clock-work. Says he must have it or he can't sleep a wink."

Mr. Anderson and Mr. O'Brien said nothing in reply, but they looked very thoughtful, and even sad, as the skipper dropped the sail and came alongside the pier. He carried the joke a little too far. MAX ADELER.

THANATOPSIS.

To him who in the love of Nature holds
Communion with her visible forms, she speaks
A various language; for his gayer hours
She has a voice of gladness, and a smile
And eloquence of beauty; and she glides
Into his darker musings, with a mild
And healing sympathy, that steals away
Their sharpness, ere he is aware.

When thoughts
Of the last bitter hour come like a blight
Over thy spirit, and sad images
Of the stern agony, and shroud, and pall,
And breathless darkness, and the narrow house,
Make thee to shudder, and grow sick at heart;—
Go forth, under the open sky, and list
To Nature's teachings, while from all around—
Earth and her waters, and the depths of air—
Comes a still voice:

Yet a few days, and thee
The all-beholding sun shall see no more
In all his course; nor yet in the cold ground,
Where thy pale form is laid with many tears,
Nor in the embrace of ocean, shall exist
Thy image. Earth that nourished thee, shall claim
Thy growth, to be resolved to earth again,
And, lost each human trace, surrendering up

Thine individual being, shalt thou go
To mix forever with the elements—
To be a brother to the insensible rock,
And to the sluggish clod, which the rude swain
Turns with his share, and treads upon. The oak
Shall send his roots abroad, and pierce thy mold.

Yet not to thine eternal resting-place
Shalt thou retire alone—nor couldst thou wish
Couch more magnificent. Thou shalt lie down
With patriarchs of the infant world—with kings,
The powerful of the earth—the wise, the good,
Fair forms, and hoary seers, of ages past,
All in one mighty sepulcher. The hills
Rock-ribbed, and ancient as the sun—the vales
Stretching in pensive quietness between;
The venerable woods—rivers that move
In majesty, and the complaining brooks
That make the meadows green; and, poured round all,
Old ocean's gray and melancholy waste—
Are but the solemn decorations all
Of the great tomb of man.

The golden sun,
The planets, all the infinite host of heaven,
Are shining on the sad abodes of death,
Through the still lapse of ages. All that tread
The globe are but a handful to the tribes
That slumber in its bosom. Take the wings
Of morning, and the Barcan desert pierce,
Or lose thyself in the continuous woods
Where rolls the Oregon, and hears no sound
Save his own dashings—yet the dead are there;
And millions in those solitudes, since first
The flight of years began, have laid them down
In their last sleep—the dead there reign alone.

So shalt thou rest—and what if thou withdraw
Unheeded by the living—and no friend
Take note of thy departure?   All that breathe
Will share thy destiny.   The gay will laugh
When thou art gone, the solemn brood of care
Plod on, and each one, as before, will chase
His favorite phantom; yet all these shall leave
Their mirth and their employments, and shall come
And make their bed with thee.

                    As the long train
Of ages glide away, the sons of men,
The youth in life's green spring, and he who goes
In the full strength of years, matron, and maid,
And the sweet babe, and the gray-headed man—
Shall one by one be gathered to thy side,
By those who, in their turn, shall follow them.

  So live, that when thy summons comes to join
The innumerable caravan, that moves
To that mysterious realm, where each shall take
His chamber in the silent halls of death,
Thou go not, like the quarry-slave, at night,
Scourged to his dungeon, but, sustained and soothed
By an unfaltering trust, approach thy grave,
Like one who wraps the drapery of his couch
About him, and lies down to pleasant dreams.
                    WILLIAM CULLEN BRYANT.

RUTH.

She was a thing of grace; her movements were the poetry of motion, and her eyes were soft and mellow enough to throw any fanciful mind into an ecstasy of pleasure. She was beautifully pale, coyly shy, and languorously spirituelle. No Gainsborough hat tilted jauntily on the side of her head; no blushing rose, lit with the liquid pearls of night, found a warm nest in her ringlets; no fragrant sandalwood fan was open before her eyes, and no Marie Antoinette slipper graced her small, crescent-like foot.

She was the picture of rustic sweetness and simplicity, as she stood among the roses that shed their subtle perfume round the porch. She walked to the gate and looked anxiously down the road, as though her susceptible soul was cradled in expectation, and, seeing no one approach, she returned to the stoop, but didn't engage her mind in the perusal of the latest novel. She didn't, as others often do, go into raptures over "Phillis," "Airy Fairy Lillian," or other books equally ridiculous. She never read novels at all—not even "The House of Secrets;" and, strange as it may seem, cared little for music, even the compositions of Bellini and Donizetti. She never went to the opera, and found little harmony in the tremulous music of a mandolin; and she was even unacquainted with the poems of Dobson, Aldrich, Mortimer Collins, and Owen Meredith.

It is very likely that no one ever saw a girl with her peculiar ideas. She had no ambition to go on the stage, and become a rival of Clara Morris; she never desired to gain immortal fame as a writer of magazine verses, or a compiler of fashion notes. She was never known to take an active part in a church fair, or to work slippers or smoking-caps for the minister. She was never present at the opening of a dry-goods store, and could be no more rejoiced at the prospect of a 77-cent sale than could an artist on being presented with a jeweled cimeter.

Needle-work found in her no warm admirer, and decorative art was as far from her idea of the beautiful as one could well imagine. Variations in the fashions never troubled her. She little cared whether the kid gloves most in vogue were four or fourteen-buttoned. She never filled books with various autumn leaves, as do many young ladies whose minds incline to the sentimental side of life; and she never was known to rush upon a gentleman visitor and exclaim:

"Now, Mr. Thompson, just see my new autograph album. Don't you think it is just too awfully cute for anything?"

No, she was never guilty of such a social subterfuge—a subterfuge so called because the act is usually followed by a request that something be written in the album. She never sketched or painted, though it must be confessed that she delighted in pretty idylic pictures set in the frame of summer. She was fond of billowy, fragrant clover, and roses, and anemones, and running brooks, and waving ferns. She was also fond of pet dogs, and would run around the garden in happy spirits with them barking at her heels.

It was the opinion of every one in the neighborhood that Ruth was a very peculiar composition of incongruities. No young gentleman cared about taking her to picnics or parties, and there was very little rivalry over her. But there was one thing every one admired in her, and that was her very high and dignified sense of propriety in all things. She was always about right, too. She would never correct a young man's grammar before a company. She would never leave church during the sermon; she would never enter church half an hour after the beginning of the services to exhibit her new hat to the congregation.

Ruth was a model in many ways. While I have been digressing on her virtues and alleged vices, she has decided to walk to the woods, her spirit full of reverie, and her reverie full of the sunshine and glory of a summer dream. Slowly she moves down the lane, without parasol or gloves, and seems like an airy creation of Elf-land. She hums a song after her own fashion while on her journey. After reaching the woods, she searches out her favorite bower beside the margin of a rippling brook —a bower in which Titania might recline intoxicated with lute-notes and aromatic zephyrs. And here she pauses, and reclines her graceful figure on the delightful moss, and floats to a realm of violets and visions, where fairies play on mandolins in flower-bells, and all is buried in the hush of a purple after-glow. Thus she dreams until wakened by some small boys who have come to drive her home. Ruth is a goat.   R. K. MUNKITTRICK.

LINES ON A SKELETON.

Behold this ruin! 'Twas a skull
Once of ethereal spirit full.
This narrow cell was Life's retreat,
This space was Thought's mysterious seat.
What beauteous visions filled this spot!
What dreams of pleasure long forgot!
Nor Hope, nor Joy, nor Love, nor Fear,
Have left one trace of record here.

Beneath this moldering canopy,
Once shone the bright and busy eye;
But start not at the dismal void—
If social love that eye employed,
If with no lawless fire it gleamed,
But through the dews of kindness beamed,
That eye shall be forever bright
When stars and sun are sunk in night.

Within this hollow cavern hung
The ready, swift, and tuneful tongue.
If falsehood's honey it disdained,
And when it could not praise, was chained,
If bold in Virtue's cause it spoke,
Yet gentle concord never broke!
This silent tongue shall plead for thee
When time unvails Eternity.

Say, did these fingers delve the mine?
Or with the envied rubies shine?
To hew the rock or wear the gem
Can little now avail to them.
But if the page of truth they sought,
Or comfort to the mourner brought,
These hands a richer meed shall claim
Than all that wait on Wealth or Fame.

Avails it, whether bare or shod,
These feet the path of duty trod?
If from the bowers of Ease they fled,
To seek Affliction's humble shed;
If Grandeur's guilty bribe they spurned,
And home to Virtue's cot returned,
These feet with angels' wings shall vie,
And tread the palace of the sky.

ANONYMOUS.

THE FRESHMAN'S STORY.

When the old farmer came into the car, the only vacant seat was that beside a freshman who was reading a book. The old man wanted to be sociable, and patiently he said to the freshman:

"You're fond of novels, I reckon?"

"I? no," said the young man. "This isn't a novel. It is Hume's account of the 'Siege of Troy.'"

"Troy, hey? I know all about that town. What's the book say in reference to it?"

"Why, you know the whole trouble was caused by a woman named Helen, who——"

"Any last name?"

"No; she was——"

"Did she go to the Presbyterian Church? A small woman with one eye a little warped? I'll bet anything I know that woman!"

"And you know," said the freshman, with a far-away look in his eyes, "she came to Troy and went to live with Priam, who——"

"Prime! I knew a Ferguson who married a Prime. He was in the the truck business in Syracuse; had relations in Troy, most likely."

"Helen's husband persuaded the Greeks to come with him to Troy to try to get her back again, and so they manned their ships and sailed toward the city."

"Came up in the night boat, did they?"

"Oh, no; it is believed that they used their oars over the entire distance."

"Rowed up! Nobody but a lot of jackasses would have done that when they could have come right up the river shore on an express train."

"As soon as they landed, the people of Troy closed the gates of the city, and——"

"What for?"

"To keep them out, of course."

"Alley gates or front gates?"

"What?"

"Go on; it makes no difference. I keep my back gate fastened, myself, on account of tramps. I suppose the——"

"The Greeks were led by a number of brave soldiers. Among these was Ulysses, who——"

"Who did you say?"

"Ulysses, the——"

"See a here, young man, you're not telling the truth! Don't I know that Grant never came to Troy to fool with anybody's front gate! You ought to be ashamed of yourself to try to impose on a man who is old enough to be your grandfather!"

"You don't understand. I mean that——"

"If a man don't want him for a third term, well and good; but there's no use of putting things on him that he never did."

The freshman seemed to be absorbed in examining the landscape from the window.

"And the leader of the Trojans," he said, "was a man named Hector. And he came out and stood on the wall, to observe the——"

"Bricklayer, was he?"

"A soldier, and when the Greeks came up they demanded that he should surrender Helen to her husband."

"Why didn't he take out a writ of *haebaes corpus*? I know the judge in Troy. He'd a handed that woman over quicker 'n a wink."

"Hector would not consent to give her up, and then the fighting began. They fought, and fought, and fought outside the city limits."

"Well," said the old man, "I don't like to doubt your word, my son, but it's mighty queer there was nothing about the fuss in any of the papers. Where were the police?"

"And one day, when the Trojans were all within the city, Ulysses came up to the gate, and, picking up a huge stone weighing three hundred pounds, he hurled it at——"

"Stop! Stop right there! How much did you say that stone weighed?"

"Three or four hundred pounds."

"And Grant picked it up?"

"I said Ulysses picked it up, and with it he burst the gate to splinters."

"So young, and yet so wicked," said the old man, sadly. "My son, what you want is a terrible lot of moral discipline, laid on thick and rubbed in hard. I never heard your equal at fiction."

"Well," said the freshman, examining the 74th page of his book, and apparently not heeding the old man, "after a number of combats Hector came out one day, and he and Achilles had a fight all by themselves."

"With gloves?"

"And when they had exchanged a good many blows, Hector started to run, and he ran clear around Troy three times with Achilles in close pursuit."

"Young man, if you don't stop that kind of thing, I'll change my seat! You couldn't make me believe that any man had as good wind as that, if you were under oath."

"On the third lap Achilles overtook him, and killed him on the spot."

"Did the case come before the grand jury?"

"But this, you know, did not let the Greeks into the city. And how do you think they finally got in?"

"Took the horse-cars?"

"Of course not."

"Marched in in a torchlight procession?"

"No."

"Came in the band-wagon of a circus?"

"No; they made a wooden horse, hollow, and——"

"Made a wooden horse holloa! There you go again! Why don't you give up that bad habit of violating the truth?"

"And they put a band of men inside the horse who——"

"Rocking horse, did you say?"

"Who laid low until the horse got into the city, when they sprang out, opened the gates. let in their friends, and then the whole party burned the city to ashes."

The old man looked anxiously at the freshman. He seemed hurt and offended by the youth's depravity. Then he said, mournfully:

"And when do you say all this happened?"

"About three thousand years ago."

The aged man buried his face in his hands and groaned.

"Why, you phenomenal liar! Don't I *know* that Troy was founded upon the banks of the Hudson later than 1786."

The train stopped, and the freshman rose to get out. As he went through the door of the car, the old farmer leaned over the man in the seat in front of him and said:

"See that boy going out there?'

"Yes."

"Well, what he wants is about eight thousand years of steady going to Sunday-school. He can outlie any boy of his size in the temperate zone."   MAX ADELER.

JUST ONE.

Just one little cloudlet, a miniature trifle,
  Just one little spot on the bright shining sun;
Just one little blemish, a sunbeam to rifle,
  And yet in that moment the storm had begun.

Just one little splash on the fair bosomed river,
  Just one little rain-drop, succeeded by more;
Just one throb responsive deep waters deliver,
  Then to passionate heaving and swaying give o'er.

Just one little flaw 'neath the clear alabaster,
  Hath many a beautiful figure defaced;
Just one rapturous moment hath wrought grave disaster,
  And fashioned a blot which could ne'er be erased.

Just one fairy castle, in innocence builded,
  Whate'er its foundation, 'twas fair to behold;
Its halls were of faith, and its panels were gilded
  With a trust that its object in grace did infold.

Just one little blow and the castle lay shattered,
  Almost without effort 'twas felled to the earth;
Its doors were unhinged and its windows were battered;
  Lo! A grief to the heart that had given it birth.

Just one ray of hope, and the torch was relighted,
  Which pointed whereby had such rule occurred;
Just one beacon light, and no longer benighted,
  A chord of true, fervent devotion was stirred.

Just one swift resolve to avert coming sorrow,
  One quick flash of thought, which allotted its due,
Doth yield deep content, which another may borrow,
  And never have cause the insignia to rue.

Just one little prayer, winging softly toward heaven,
  A fluttering breath, like a wandering waif;
Just one trembling tear-drop runs counter the leaven,
  And the murmur re-echoes, "Thank God, we are safe."

AZALEA E. OSGOOD.

SPEAK NO ILL.

Nay, speak no ill! a kindly word
  Can never leave a sting behind,
And, oh! to breathe each tale we've heard
  Is far beneath a noble mind.
Full oft a better seed is sown
  By choosing thus the kinder plan;
For if little good be known,
  Still let us speak the best we can.

Give me the heart that fain would hide,
  Would fain another's fault efface;
How can it please our human pride,
  To prove humanity but base?
No; let us reach a higher mood,
  A noble estimate of man;
Be earnest in search for good,
  And speak of all the best we can.

Then speak no ill, but lenient be
  To other's failings as your own;
If you're the first a fault to see,
  Be not the first to make it known;
For life is but a passing day,
  No lip can tell how brief its span;
Then, oh! the little time we stay,
  Let's speak of all the best we can.

CHARLES SWAIN.

ODE TO MY LITTLE SON.

Thou happy, happy elf!
(But stop—first let me kiss away that tear!)
Thy tiny image of myself!
(My love, he's poking peas into his ear!)
Thou merry, laughing sprite!
With spirits, feather light,
Untouched by sorrow, and unsoiled by sin,
(Good heavens! the child is swallowing a pin!)

Thou little tricksy Puck!
With antic toys so funnily bestuck,
Light as the singing bird that wings the air,
(The door! the door! he'll tumble down the stair!)
Thou darling of thy sire!
(Why, Jane, he'll set his pinafore afire!)
Thou imp of mirth and joy!
In love's dear chain so strong and bright a link,
Thou idol of thy parents (Drat the boy!
There goes my ink!)

Thou cherub—but of earth;
Fit playfellow for Fays by moonlight pale,
In harmless sport and mirth,
(That dog will bite him, if he pulls his tail!)
Thou human humming-bee, extracting honey
From every blossom in the world that blows,
Singing in youth's Elysium ever funny,
(Another tumble—that's his precious nose!)
Thy father's pride and hope!
(He'll break the mirror with that skipping-rope!)
With pure heart newly stamped from nature's mint,
(Where did he learn that squint!)

Thou young domestic dove!
(He'll have that jug off with another shove!)
    Dear nursling of the hymeneal nest!
    (Are those torn clothes his best?)
    Little epitome of man!
(He'll climb upon the table, that's his plan!)
Touched with the beauteous tints of dawning life,
    (He's got a knife!)
    Thou enviable being!
No storms, no clouds, in thy blue sky foreseeing,
    Play on, play on,
    My elfin John!

Toss the light ball—bestride the stick,
(I knew so many cakes would make him sick!)
With fancies buoyant as the thistle-down,
Prompting the face grotesque, and antic brisk
    With many a lamb-like frisk,
(He's got the scissors, snipping at your gown!)
    Thou pretty opening rose!
(Go to your mother, child, and wipe your nose!)
Balmy, and breathing music like the south,
(He really brings my heart into my mouth!)
Fresh as the morn, and brilliant as its star,
(I wish that window had an iron bar!)
Bold as a hawk, yet gentle as a dove,
(I'll tell you what, my love,
I cannot write, unless he's sent above!)

                  THOMAS HOOD.

THE SURPRISE PARTY.

John Pinchbeck lived on Murray Hill,
   The upper-crust among;
He had a healthy bank account,
   His wife was fair and young.
He earned a handsome competence
   By selling hides and leather;
His head was level, and his heart
   As light as any feather.

But John's wife, pretty though she was,
   And sociable and free;
Was fond of taking on French airs,
   When in society.
To see the lady in her silks
   And diamonds arrayed
'Twas hard to b'lieve she once had been
   A simple dairy maid.

But so it was—and one fine day
   A couple stout and jolly—
Zeke Soper and his wife came down
   To see their darling Polly.
For Polly was the lady's name,
   When at her spinning-wheel,
But now she'd changed it to Pauline,
   As being more genteel.

"Oh, lawful sakes!" Zeke's wife cried out,
   When she the mansion stood in,
"I hope I never more may see
   A bowl of hasty puddin'.
If this ain't scrumshious! Only see
   The picters on the ceilin'!
As nat'ral as life! Why, Zeke,
   I'm on the p'int o' squealin'!

"It's fresco, is it?   Well, I vow,
   I'm drefful glad you told me!
And see the carpets and the cheers,
   And sofys!   Zeke, hold me!
I'm nigh a bustin' with amaze!
   I really am!   Why, Polly,
With all these fixin's 'round you, gal,
   You must be awful jolly!

"It's mighty fine!   But, goodness me,
   Zeke, see them naked figgers
A-standing on the mantel-piece;
   They make me blush; by jiggers!
You say they're noble works of art,
   And great folks come to view 'em?
Well, Polly dear, if I was you
   I'd put some clothes onto 'em.

"What's that you say?   Pauline's your name
   Good gracious me, what folly!
Why, weren't I by, you silly thing,
   When you was christened Polly?
And if the name was good enough
   For your dear, blessed mother,
It's good enough for you, and I
   Sha'n't call you any other.

"But, speaking of your christnin', Poll,
   To me it is bewilderin'
That you've been married seven years
   And ain't had any children.
Your ma had twelve and I've had eight—
   Now, Polly dear, confess it,
A house, though grand, ain't worth a snap,
   Without a babe to bless it.

But, deary me, I'm tired out!
  My bones are ackin' cruel—
Come, Polly, show us to our room—
  I'd like a bowl of gruel.
And can't you get some boneset tea,
  And mustard for a body,
And a warm hand iron for my feet?
  And Zeke would like some toddy!

*   *   *   *   *

Next evening, Mrs. Pinchbeck thus
  Addressed her lord and master:
"Oh, husband, how can we survive
  This terrible disaster?
I'll die—I know I shall—if aunt
  And uncle with us tarry
Till they are seen by proud Miss Sharp
  And jealous Mrs. Barry.

"Such a disgrace!   Just think of it!
  This morning at the table,
The servants, though afraid to laugh
  Aloud, were scarcely able
To hide their mirth, when Uncle Zeke,
  By Aunt Jerusha followed,
Picked up the half-filled finger bowl
  And all the water swallowed!

Just then the hall-bell rang aloud,
  And soon a summons hearty
Smote on the lady' sstartled ear,
  "Ha! Pinchbeck! Here's a party!
We've come to give you a surprise,
  We know you'll be delighted—
And welcome us right cordially,
  Though we were not invited?"

Poor Mrs. Pinchbeck!   How was she
   The dreadful blow to parry?
She heard the voices of her friends,
   Miss Sharp and Mrs. Barry.
And many others whom she knew
   Delighted to perplex her,
And who would rummage high and low
   To scandalize and vex her.

"Friends!" cried the lady, "welcome all—
   I'm glad to see you, really!
Just pass down to the dining-room
   And use the closets freely—
But please don't come up stairs, for we
   Two friends are entertaining—
Distinguished persons from abroad—
   Both nervous and complaining!

Oh, horror!   Even as she spoke,
   A voice that made her shiver
Came from above, "Oh, Zeke!" it cried
   "That sirup for my liver!
I've left it in the room below—
   I cannot do without it—
Besides, there's company down stairs—
   Let's go and ask about it!"

Ere Mrs. Pinchbeck could prevent
   The act that her degraded,
The aged couple merrily
   The dining-room invaded.
To make the matter worse, old Zeke
   Had taken too much toddy,
And felt that he was just as rich
   And grand as anybody.

"Why, how d' due, good folks!" he cried,
　And then at Mrs. Barry
He winked and said facetiously,
　"Lord, what a spread you carry!
Well, make yourselves to hum at once!
　Away with melancholy;
Hurrah!　Let's have a straight-four dance!
　Jerushy, where is Polly?

"She needn't keep herself so shy
　Because she's got a fortun',
She was as poor as any one
　'Fore Pinchbeck did his courtin'—
But this I'll always say for Poll—
　No other gal, I reckon,
Could ekal her at dairy work,
　At washin' or at bakin'.

Ah, here she is! and Pinchbeck, too!
　Come, folks, bring on your fiddle,
And let us have an old-time dance,
　'Up sides and down the middle.
Come Polly, put your best licks in,
　Just as you used to do it,
At all our frolics down to hum—
　Go on, I'll see yeou through it!"

Thus Uncle Zekel rattled on,
　And when his tongue had tired,
Old Aunt Jerush took up the theme,
　With emulation fired.
She told her niece's history,
　From childhood till she married,
While Mrs. Pinchbeck helpless stood,
　And not a thrust was parried.

Let's close the scene—a week passed by—
　　The Pinchbecks, half demented,
Were writhing still when they received
　　A note with perfume scented,
From Mrs. Barry. Thus it read:
　' " To Mrs. Pinchbeck greeting:
Dear friend—the ladies of our set
　　Are soon to have a meeting.

" Our object is to call upon
　　And speak with Madame Herman,
About the getting up in style
　　Of our forthcoming german.
And if you'll send us the address
　　Of your high-bred relations,
I'll see that they as well as you,
　　Are granted invitations."

The moral of my story is
　　That pride must have a tumble—
That those who in their wealth forget
　　They once were poor and humble—
Who think they wear so close a mask,
　　That no one can detect it,
May come to grief with all their airs,
　　E'en when they least expect it.

FRANCIS S. SMITH

THE MEN TO MAKE A STATE.

The men to make a state must be intelligent men. I do not mean that they must know that two and two make four; or, that six per cent. a year is half per cent a month. I take a wider and a higher range. I limit myself to no mere utilitarian intelligence. This has its place. And this will come almost unsought. The contact of the rough and rugged world will *force* men to it in self-defense. The lust of worldly gain will drag men to it in self-aggrandizement. But men *so* made, will never make a state. The intelligence which that demands will take a wider and a higher range. Its study will be man. It will make history its cheap experience. It will read hearts. It will know men. It will first know *itself*. What else can govern men? Who else can know the men to *govern* men? The right of suffrage is a fearful thing. It calls for wisdom, and discretion, and intelligence, of no ordinary standard. It takes in, at every exercise, the interests of all the nation. Its results reach forward through time into eternity. Its discharge must be accounted for among the dread responsibilities of the great day of judgment. Who will go to it blindly? Who will go to it passionately? Who will go to it, as a sycophant, a tool, a slave? How many *do!* *These* are not the men to make a state.

The men to make a state must be honest men. I do not mean men that would never *steal*. I do not mean men that would scorn to cheat in making change. I mean men with a single *face*. I mean men with a single *eye*. I mean men with a single *tongue*. I mean men that consider always what is *right;* and to do it at whatever cost. I mean men who can dine, like Andrew Marvel, on a neck of mutton; and whom, therefore, no king on earth can *buy*. Men that are in the market for the highest bidder; men that make politics their *trade*, and look to office for a *living*; men that

will crawl, where they cannot climb; *these* are not the men
to make a state.

The men, to make a state, must be brave men. I do not
mean men that pick a *quarrel*. I do not mean the men
that carry *dirks*. I do not mean the men that call themselves hard names; as Bouncers, Killers, and the like. I
mean the men that walk with open face and unprotected
breast. I mean the men that *do*, but do not *talk*. I mean
the men that dare to stand alone. I mean the men that are
to-day where they were *yesterday*, and *will* be 'there *to-morrow*. I mean the men that can stand still and take the
storm. I mean the men that are afraid to *kill*, but not
afraid to *die*. The man that calls hard names and uses
threats; the man that stabs, in secret, with his tongue or
with his pen; the man that moves a mob to deeds of violence and self-destruction; the man that freely offers his
last drop of blood, but never sheds the *first; these* are not
the men to make a state.

The men to make a state must be religious men. States
are from God. States are dependent upon God. States are
accountable to God. To leave God out of states, is to be
Atheists. I do not mean that men must *cant*. I do not
mean that men must wear long faces. I do not mean that
men must talk of *conscience*, while they take your *spoons*.
One shrewdly called hypocrisy, the tribute which vice pays
to virtue. These masks and visors, in like manner, are
the forced concession which a moral nature makes him,
whom, at the same time, it dishonors. I speak of men
who feel and own a God. I speak of men who feel and
own their sins. I speak of men who think the Cross no
shame. I speak of men who have it in their heart as well
as on their brow. The men that own no future, the men
that trample on the Bible, the men that never pray, are
not the men to make a *state*.

The men, to make a state, are made by faith. A man
that has no faith, is so much *flesh*. His heart, *a muscle;*

nothing more. He has no *past* for *reverence;* no *future* for *reliance.* He lives. So does a clam. Both die. Such men can never make a state. There must be *faith,* which furnishes the fulcrum Archimedes could not find, for the long lever that should move the world. There must be faith to look through clouds and storms up to the sun that shines as cheerily on high as on creation's morn. There must be faith that can lay hold of heaven, and let the earth swing from beneath it, if God will. There must be faith that can afford to sink the *present* in the *future;* and let *time* go, in its strong grasp upon *eternity.* This is the way that men are made to make a state.

The men to make a state are made by self-denial. The willow dallies with the water, and is fanned forever by its coolest breeze, and draws its waves up in continual pulses of refreshment and delight; and is a *willow,* after all. An acorn has been loosened, some autumnal morning, by a squirrel's foot. It finds a nest in some rude cleft of an old granite rock, where there is scarcely earth to cover it. It knows no shelter, and it feels no shade. It squares itself against the storms. It shoulders through the blast. It *asks* no favor, and *gives* none. It grapples with the rock. It crowds up toward the sun. It is an oak. It has been seventy years an oak. It *will* be an oak for *seven times* seventy years; unless you need a man-of-war to thunder at the foe that shows a flag upon the shore, where freemen dwell; and then you take no willow in its daintiness and gracefulness; but that old, hardy, storm-stayed and storm-strengthened oak. So are the men made that will make a state.

The men to make a state are themselves made by obedience. Obedience is the health of human hearts; obedience to God; obedience to father and to mother, who are, to children, in the place of God; obedience to teachers and to masters, who are in the place of father and of mother; obedience to spiritual pastors, who are God's

ministers; and the powers that be, which are ordained of
God. Obedience is but self-government in action; and he
can never govern men who does not govern first himself.
Only such men can make a state. GEORGE W. DOANE.

MOTHER AND CHILD.

Drunk and disorderly—so it was said,
Into the court-room the culprit was led;
There on her dark and unwomanly face
Lingered the signs of her shame and disgrace,
Soiled with the mud in whose depths she had lain—
All the sweet instincts of modesty slain—
 Standing so boldly there,
 Waiting so coldly there,
Hearing her sentence with sullen disdain.

Sternly the justice looked down from his seat—
Down at the woman who stood at his feet;
Wondering how she had wandered so far
From the clear heights where the virtuous are.
Ah, how unlovely she seemed in the gloom,
There in that dismal and crowded court-room,
 Treading unthinkingly,
 Going unshrinkingly
On to the depths of her terrible doom!

Suddenly, strangely, his features grew mild,
There on her breast lay a pure little child,
Smiling at him with such innocent eyes,
Blue in their depths as the bonny blue skies.
Over her shoulder it struggled to climb,
Sweetly unconscious of sorrow or crime,
 Laughing so merrily,
 Beautiful, verily—
Fair as a lily-bud found in the slime.

Softly he spoke to the woman—and then
Out from that dim, noisy court-room again
Bore she her baby, with faltering tread—
Freed for the sake of that innocent head.
Just for a moment the bonny wee child
Backward looked, over her shoulder and smiled;
   Lying so sweetly there—
   Cursed so completely there,
By the foul touch of those fingers defiled.

Sadly the justice bent over his book,
Asking himself, as he thought of that look,
Through what dark pathways of sin and deceit
Fortune would carry those small, winsome feet.
Ah, that a blossom so tender should rest,
There on that hard and unwomanly breast!
   One so undutiful
   Crowned with the beautiful!
Sin by the glory of motherhood blest.

Think of it, fathers, when sweet eyes of brown
Watch through the window your coming from town.
Plump little feet patter over the floor,
Eager to meet your warm kiss at the door;
Tiny wee hands draw your chair to its place—
Fairy-like forms clamber up to your face—
   Cherished so carefully,
   Nurtured so prayerfully,
Kept from all knowledge of shame or disgrace.

Dream of it mothers, when lullabies sung
Over the cradle so tenderly swung
Blend with the laugh of the baby that lies
Warm in the light of your watchful blue eyes.
Ah, but how proudly you guard her from harm,

Keeping her safe from all thought of alarm—
   Kissing, caressing her,
   Lovingly pressing her
Close to your heart in your sheltering arm.
                 NELLY B. SIMMONS.

A RILL FROM THE TOWN PUMP.

At this sultry noontide, I am cupbearer to the parched populace, for whose benefit an iron goblet is chained to my waist. Like a dram seller on the mall, at muster day, I cry aloud to all and sundry, in my plainest accents, and at the very tip-top of my voice. Here it is, gentlemen! Here is the good liquor! Walk up, walk up, gentlemen, walk up, walk up! Here is the superior stuff! Here is the unadulterated ale of Father Adam —better than Cognac, Holland, Jamaica, strong beer, or wine of any price; here it is by the hogshead or single glass, and not a cent to pay! Walk up, gentlemen, walk up, and help yourselves! It were a pity, if all this outcry should draw no customers. Here they come. A hot day, gentlemen! Quaff, and away again, so as to keep yourselves in a nice, cool sweat.

Welcome, most rubicund sir! You and I have been great strangers hitherto; nor, to confess the truth, will my nose be anxious for a closer intimacy, till the fumes of your breath be a little less potent. Mercy on you, man! the water absolutely hisses down! Fill again, and tell me, on the word of an honest toper, did you ever, in cellar, tavern, or any kind of dram shop, spend the price of your children's food, for a swig half so delicious? Now, for the first time these ten years, you know the flavor of cold water. Good-by; and, whenever you are thirsty, remember that I keep a constant supply, at the old stand.

Who next? Oh, my little friend, you are let loose from

school, and come hither to scrub your blooming face, and drown the memory of certain taps of the ferule, and other schoolboy troubles. in a draught from the Town Pump. Take it, pure as the current of your young life. Take it, and may your heart and tongue never be scorched with a fiercer thirst than now. There, my dear child, put down the cup, and yield your place to this elderly gentleman, who treads so tenderly over the paving stones, that I suspect he is afraid of breaking them.

What! he limps by, without so much as thanking me, as if my hospitable offers were meant only for people who have no wine cellars. Well, well, sir; no harm done, I hope! Go, draw the cork, tip the decanter; but, when your great toe shall set you a-roaring, it will be no affair of mine. This thirsty dog, with red tongue lolling out, does not scorn my hospitality, but stands on his hind legs, and laps eagerly out of the trough. See how lightly he capers away again. Jowler, did your worship ever have the gout? Are you all satisfied? Then wipe your mouths, my good friends; and, while my spout has a moment's leisure, I will delight the town with a few historical reminiscences.

In far antiquity, beneath a darksome shadow of venerable boughs, a spring bubbled out of the leaf-strewn earth, in the very spot where you now behold me, on the sunny pavement. But, in the course of time, a Town Pump was sunk into the source of the ancient spring; and, when the first decayed, another took its place—and then another, and still another—till here stand I, gentlemen and ladies, to serve you with my iron goblet. Drink, and be refreshed! The water is pure and cold as that which slacked the thirst of the red sagamore, beneath the aged boughs, though now the gem of the wilderness is treasured under these hot stones, where no shadow falls, but from the brick buildings. And be it the moral of my story, that, as this wasted and long-lost fountain is now known and prized again, so shall the virtues of cold water, too little valued since your father's days, be recognized by all.

Your pardon, good people! I must interrupt my stream of eloquence, and spout forth a stream of water, to replenish the trough for this teamster and his two yoke of oxen, who have come from Topsfield, or somewhere along that way. No part of my business is pleasanter than the watering of cattle. Look! how rapidly they lower the watermark on the sides of the trough, till their capacious stomachs are moistened with a gallon or two apiece, and they can afford time to breathe it in, with sighs of calm enjoyment. Now they roll their quiet eyes around the brim of their monstrous drinking vessels. An ox is your true toper.

But I perceive, my dear auditors, that you are impatient for the remainder of my discourse. Impute it, I beseech you, to no defect of modesty, if I insist a little longer on so fruitful a topic as my own multifarious merits. It is altogether for your good. The better you think of me, the better men and women you will find yourselves. I shall say nothing of my all-important aid on washing days; though, on that account alone, I might call myself the household god of a hundred families. Far be it from me, also, to hint, my respectable friends, at the show of dirty faces, which you would present, without my pains to keep you clean.

Nor will I remind you how often, when the midnight bells make you tremble for your combustible town, you have fled to the Town Pump, and found me always at my post, firm, amid the confusion, and ready to drain my vital current in your behalf. Neither is it worth while to lay much stress on my claims to a medical diploma, as the physician, whose simple rule of practice is preferable to all the nauseous lore which has found men sick or left them so, since the days of Hippocrates. Let us take a broader view of my beneficial influence on mankind.

No! these are trifles, compared with the merits which wise men concede to me—if not in my single self, yet as the representative of a class—of being the grand reformer of the age. From my spout, and such spouts as mine, must flow the stream that shall cleanse our 'earth of the vast portion of its crime and anguish, which has gushed from the fiery fountains of the still. In this mighty enterprise, the cow shall be my great confederate. Milk and water! The Town Pump and the Cow! Such is the glorious co-partnership that shall tear down the distilleries and brewhouses, uproot the vineyards, shatter the cider-presses, ruin the tea and coffee trade, and, finally, monopolize the whole business of quenching thirst. Blessed consummation!

Ahem! Dry work, this speechifying; especially to an unpracticed orator. I never conceived till now, what toil the temperance lecturers undergo for my sake. Hereafter, they shall have the business to themselves. Do, some kind Christian, pump a stroke or two, just to wet my whistle. Thank you, sir! My dear hearers, when the world shall have been regenerated, by my instrumentality, you will collect your useless vats and liquor casks into one great pile, and make a bonfire, in honor of the Town Pump. And, when I shall have decayed, like my predecessors, then, if you revere my memory, let a marble fountain, richly sculptured, take my place upon the spot.

NATHANIEL HAWTHORNE.

THE BLIND BOY'S SPEECH.

Think not that blindness makes me sad,
My thoughts, like yours, are often glad,
Parents I have, who love me well,
Their different voices I can tell.
Though far away from them, I hear,
In dreams, their music meets my ear,
Is there a star so dear above
As the low voice of one you love?

I never saw my father's face,
Yet on his forehead when I place
My hand, and feel the wrinkles there,
Left less by time than anxious care,
I fear the world has sights of *woe*,
To knit the brows of manhood so—
I sit upon my father's knee;
He'd loved me *less*, if I could see.

I never saw my mother smile;
Her gentle tones my heart beguile.
They fall like distant melody—
They are so mild and sweet to me.
She murmurs not—my mother dear!
Though sometimes I have kissed the tear
From her soft cheek, to tell the joy
One smiling word would give her boy.

Right merry was I every day!
Fearless to run about and play
With sisters, brothers, friends, and all—
To answer to their sudden call,
To join the ring, to speed the chase,
To find each playmate's hiding-place,
And pass my hand across his brow,
To tell him I could do it now!

Yet, though delightful flew the hours,
So passed in childhood's peaceful bowers,
When all were gone to school but I,
I used to sit at home and sigh;
* And, though I never longed to view
The earth so green, the sky so blue,
I thought I'd give the world to look
Along the pages of a book.

Now, since I learned to read and write,
My heart is filled with new delight;
And music, too −can there be found
A sight so beautiful as *sound*?
Tell me, kind friends, in one short word,
Am I not like a captive bird?
I live in song, and peace, and joy—
Though blind, a merry-hearted boy!

PARK BENJAMIN.

THE HEAVENS DECLARE THE GLORY OF GOD.

The spacious firmament on high,
With all the blue ethereal sky,
And spangled heavens, a shining flame,
Their great Original proclaim;
Th' unwearied Sun, from day to day,
Does his Creator's powers display,
And publishes to every land
The work of an Almighty hand.

Soon as the evening shades prevail,
The Moon takes up the wondrous tale,
And nightly to the listening earth,
Repeats the story of her birth;
While all the stars that round her burn,

And all the planets in their turn,
Confirm the tidings as they roll,
And spread the truth from pole to pole.

·What though, in solemn silence, all   ·
Move round the dark terrestrial ball?
What though no *real* voice or sound
Amid their radiant orbs be found?
In Reason's ear they all rejoice,
And utter forth a glorious voice,
Forever singing as they shine,
" The Hand that made us, is divine!"

JOSEPH ADDISON.

NOTHING BUT LEAVES.

Nothing but leaves; the spirit grieves
  Over a wasted life;
Sin committed while conscience slept,
Promises made but never kept,
  Hatred, battle, and strife;
    Nothing but leaves!

Nothing but leaves; no garnered sheaves
  Of life's fair, ripened grain;
Words, idle words, for earnest deeds;
We sow our seeds—lo! tares and weeds;
  We reap with toil and pain
    Nothing but leaves!

Nothing but leaves; memory weaves
  No vail to screen the past;
As we retrace our weary way,
Counting each lost and misspent day—
  We find, sadly, at last,
    Nothing but leaves!

And shall we meet the Master so,
　　Bearing our withered leaves?
The Saviour looks for perfect fruit—
We stand before him, humbled, mute;
　　Waiting the words he breathes—
　　　Nothing but leaves!

Lucy Evelina Ackerman.

LAUGH ON, LAUGH ON, TO-DAY!

Laugh on, fair cousins, for to you
　　All life is joyous yet;
Your hearts have all things to pursue,
　　And nothing to regret;
And every flower to you is fair,
　　And every month is May;
You've not been introduced to Care—
　　Laugh on, laugh on, to-day!

Old Time will fling his clouds ere long
　　Upon those sunny eyes;
The voice whose every word is song,
　　Will set itself to sighs;
Your quiet slumbers—hopes and fears
　　Will chase their rest away;
To-morrow, you'll be shedding tears—
　　Laugh on, laugh on, to-day!

Oh, yes; if any truth is found
　　In the dull schoolman's theme—
If friendship is an empty sound,
　　And love an idle dream—
If mirth, youth's playmate, feels fatigue
　　Too soon on life's long way,
At least, he'll run with you a league—
　　Laugh on, laugh on, to-day!

Perhaps your eyes may grow more bright
　　As childhood's hues depart;
You may be lovelier to the sight,
　　And dearer to the heart;
You may be sinless still, and see
　　This earth still green and gay;
But what you *are* you *will* not be,
　　Laugh on, laugh on, to-day!

O'er me have many winters crept,
　　With less of grief than joy;
But I have learned, and toiled, and wept—
　　I am no more a boy!
I've never had the gout, 'tis true,
　　My hair is hardly gray;
But now *I* cannot laugh like you;
　　Laugh on, laugh on, to-day!

I used to have as glad a face,
　　As shadowless a brow;
I once could run as blithe a race
　　As you are running now;
But never mind how *I* behave,
　　Don't interrupt your play,
And, though I look so very grave,
　　Laugh on, laugh on, to-day!

WINTHROP M. PRAED.

SPIRITUAL FREEDOM—WHAT IS IT?

I call that mind free, which masters the senses, which protects itself against animal appetites, which contemns pleasure and pain in comparison with its own energy, which penetrates beneath the body and recognizes its own reality and greatness, which passes life, not in asking what it shall eat or drink, but in hungering, thirsting, and seeking after righteousness.

I call that mind free, which escapes the bondage of matter, which, instead of stopping at the material universe, and making it a prison-wall, passes beyond it to its Author, and finds in the radiant signatures which it everywhere bears of the Infinite Spirit, helps to its own spiritual enlargement.

I call that mind free, which jealously guards its intellectual rights and powers, which calls no man master, which does not content itself with a passive or hereditary faith, which opens itself to light whencesoever it may come, which receives new truth as an angel from heaven, which, while consulting others, inquires still more of the oracle within itself, and uses instruction from abroad, not to supersede, but to quicken and exalt its own energies.

I call that mind free, which sets no bounds to its love, which is not imprisoned in itself or in a sect, which recognizes in all human beings the image of God, and the rights of His children, which delights in virtue and sympathizes with suffering, wherever they are seen, which conquers pride, anger, and sloth, and offers itself up a willing victim to the cause of mankind.

I call that mind free, which is not passively framed by outward circumstances, which is not swept away by the torrents of events, which is not the creature of accidental impulse, but which bends events to its own improvement, and acts from an inward spring, from immutable principles which it has deliberately espoused.

I call that mind free, which protects itself against the usurpations of society, which does not cower to human opinion, which feels itself accountable to a higher tribunal than man's, which respects a higher law than fashion, which respects itself too much to be the slave or tool of the many or the few.

I call that mind free, which, through confidence in God, and, in the power of virtue, has cast off all fear but that of wrong doing, which no menace or peril can enthrall, which is calm in the midst of tumults, and possesses itself, though all else be lost.

I call that mind free, which resists the bondage of habit, which does not mechanically repeat itself and copy the past, which does not live on its old virtues, which does not enslave itself to precise rules, but which forgets what is behind, listens for new and higher monitions of conscience, and rejoices to pour itself forth in fresh and higher exertions.

I call that mind free, which is jealous of its own freedom, which guards itself from being merged in others, which guards its empire over itself as nobler than the empire of the world.

In fine, *I call that mind free,* which, conscious of its affinity with God, and confiding in His promises by Jesus Christ, devotes itself faithfully to the unfolding of all its powers, which passes the bounds of time and death, which hopes to advance forever, and which finds inexhaustible power, both for action and suffering, in the prospect of immortality.   WILLIAM ELLERY CHANNING.

RING OUT THE OLD YEAR.

Ring out, wild bells, to the wild sky,
  The flying cloud, the frosty light;
  The year is dying in the night;
Ring out, wild bells, and let him die!

Ring out the old, ring in the new,
  Ring, happy bells, across the snow.
  The year is going, let him go;
Ring out the false, ring in the true!

Ring out the grief that saps the mind,
  For those that here we see no more;
  Ring out the feud of rich and poor,
Ring in redress to all mankind.

Ring out a slowly dying cause,
  And ancient forms of party strife;
  Ring in the nobler modes of life,
With sweeter manners, purer laws.

Ring out the want, the care, the sin,
  The faithless coldness of the times;
  Ring out, ring out my mournful rhymes,
But ring the fuller minstrel in.

Ring out false pride in place and blood,
  The civic slander and the spite;
  Ring in the love of truth and right,
Ring in the common love of good.

Ring out old shapes of foul disease,
  Ring out the narrowing lust of gold;
  Ring out the thousand wars of old,
Ring in the thousand years of peace.

Ring in the valiant man and free,
  The larger heart, the kindlier hand;
Ring out the darkness of the land,
  Ring in the Christ that is to be.

                              ALFRED TENNYSON.

_____

SANTA CLAUS' STOCKING.

'Twas Christmas Eve in a mining town where the great
    Sierras rise,
And many a miner "strikes it rich," and many a miner
    dies,
And a woman young and beautiful, who wore a widow's
    cap,
Sat in a lonely cabin with a bright boy on her lap.

The boy sat musing deeply till at length he raised his
    head,
And looking in the widow's eyes, he kissed her as he said,
"You say that Santa Claus won't come to-night because
    we're poor!
Why, ma, I think because of that he ought to come the
    more!

"I mean to hang my stocking up, at any rate, and try
What he will do. I do not think he'll pass our cabin by."
And then with simple, childish faith his little prayer he
    said,
Pinned his wee stocking to the jamb, kissed ma, and went
    to bed.

The widow mourned in silence, till the boy went fast
    asleep,
Then suddenly she raised her eyes above and ceased to
    weep.

"Oh, God!" she cried, "I suffer, but I know Thy ways are
    just,
Give me the total measure of my sweet boy's faith and
    trust!"

Jack Horn, a stalwart miner, brave and generous, though
    rude,
Whose ideas of propriety, to say the least, were crude,
Had meant that Christmas evening at the widow's hut to
    call,
But peeping through the window blind had heard and
    witnessed all.

A lump arose in Jack Horn's throat the while he wiped
    his eyes,
And muttered, "If I know myself I'll give you a sur-
    prise!"
Then as he looked around the place to further his design,
He spied some stockings hanging out and took one from
    the line.

And then he hurried back to camp, and to a place re-
    paired
Where miners took their precious dust and fickle fortune
    dared,
And holding up the stocking to the rough, red-shirted
    crowd,
He rapped for their attention, and then he said aloud:

"Boys, this is merry Christmas Eve, and at your door I'm
    knockin'
For slugs—this wee bag that I hold is Santa Claus'
    stockin'.
Look at it! It's as empty as the foot it fits is cunning,
I stole it from a clothes-line at the house of Poor Tom
    Dunning.

"You all knew Tom—he was, while here, as white a man
    as any,
But when death scooped him into camp he didn't leave a
    penny,
And now his widder, proud as sin, though delicate in
    figger,
Won't take a red cent from the boys, but works like any
    nigger.

"Her young kid b'lieves in Santa Claus, and he's hung up
    his stockin',
And when he finds it empty in the mornin' 'twill be
    shockin',
And so I now propose to take from every pot a shiner
And put it in this wee bag as a present from each miner."

"Done!" was the cry that then arose without a single
    croaker,
And soon the enthusiastic crowd began a game of poker.
Pot after pot was rattled off, and no man rushed to cover,
Till Santa Claus' little bag with wealth was running over.

      *   *   *   *   *   *   *

Next morn when little Tom jumped up and rushed to get
    his stocking,
As Jack Horn had predicted, its emptiness was shocking!
But he still had faith in Santa Claus, and said with visage
    bright,
"I guess he came this morning, 'cause he hadn't time last
    night.

"For I heard him on the door-step at least an hour ago,
And he's left my Christmas presents out there—he has, I
    know!"
And full of childish confidence, he opened wide the door,
And shrieked out with amazement at the wealth of things
    he saw.

A sword, a gun, a humming-top, a little rocking-chair,
A suit of clothes, some brand-new shoes, and other things
      to wear,
Hams, flour, coffee, sugar, tea, provisions, more, by far,
Than he had ever seen before, besides a shawl for ma.

He laughed, he danced, he clapped his hands, and shouted
      in his glee,
" Oh, ma, see what old Santa Claus has brought for you
      and me!
I told you he would surely come—he could not pass us
      by!"
Then suddenly he stopped and asked, "Oh, ma, what
      makes you cry?"

The widow caught close to her breast her darling, bright-
      eyed boy,
And as she kissed him tenderly, while flowed her tears of
      joy,
She said, " Oh, Heavenly Father, I have not prayed in
      vain,
And come what may hereafter, I will never doubt again!"
Again she kissed her darling and stood him on the floor,
And smoothed his curly head, and went to close the open
      door.
But an object lay before her which the cabin door was
      blocking,
And written on it legibly was "Santa Claus' stocking."

'Twas heavy, and to lift it Widow Dunning was scarce
      able,
But she managed with an effort to convey it to the table,
When she opened it and started back to find, oh, fortune
      rare!
A thousand dollars at the least, in slugs and eagles there.

A year passed by, and Jack Horn called each week on Mrs.
     Dunning;
Somehow he learned to look on her as charming, cute, and
     cunning,
And when again the Christmas time brought joy and
     bracing weather,
Jack Horn confes-ed his passion, and their lives were
     linked together.

FRANCIS S. SMITH.

FILIAL PIETY.

Filial Piety!—It is the primal bond of society—it is
that instinctive principle which, panting for its proper
good, soothes, unbidden, each sense and sensibility of man!
—it now quivers on every lip!—it now beams from every
eye!—it is an emanation of that gratitude, which, soften-
ing under the sense of recollected good, is eager to own
the vast, countless debt it ne'er, alas! can pay, for so many
long years of unceasing solicitudes, honorable self-denials,
life-preserving cares!—it is that part of our practice where
duty drops its awe!—where reverences refines into love!—
it asks no aid of memory!—it needs not the deductions of
reason!—pre-existing, paramount over all, whether law or
human rule, few arguments can increase, and none can
diminish it!—it is the *sacrament* of our nature!—not only
the duty—but the indulgence of a man—it is his first
great privilege—it is among his last, most endearing delights!—it causes the bosom to glow with reverberated
love!—it requires the visitations of nature, and returns the
blessings that have been received!—it fires emotions into
vital principle—it renders habituated instinct into a master
passion—sways all the energies of man—hangs over each
vicissitude of all that must pass away—aids the melancholy
virtues in their last sad tasks of life, to cheer the languors

of decrepitude and age—explores the thought—elucidates
the aching eye!—and breathes sweet consolation even in
the awful moment of dissolution!

RICHARD BRINSLEY SHERIDAN.

DIRGE FOR A SOLDIER.

Close his eyes; his work is done!
  What to him is friend or foeman,
Rise of moon, or set of sun,
  Hand of man, or kiss of woman?
      Lay him low, lay him low,
      In the clover or the snow;
      What cares he? he cannot know;
      Lay him low!

As man may, he fought his fight,
  Proved his truth by his endeavor;
Let him sleep in solemn night,
  Sleep forever and forever.
      Lay him low, lay him low,
      In the clover or the snow;
      What cares he? he cannot know;
      Lay him low!

Fold him in his country's stars,
  Roll the drum and fire the volley!
What to him are all our wars,
  What but death-bemocking folly?
      Lay him low, lay him low,
      In the clover or the snow;
      What cares he? he cannot know;
      Lay him low!

Leave him to God's watching eye,
  Trust him to the hand that made him,
Mortal love weeps idly by;
  God alone has power to aid him,
        Lay him low, lay him low,
        In the clover or the snow;
        What cares he? he cannot know,
        Lay him low!

                          GEORGE H. BOKER.

PERSEVERE.

Robert the Bruce in the dungeon stood,
  Waiting the hour of doom;
Behind him, the Palace of Holyrood—
  Before him, a nameless tomb.
And the foam on his lip was flecked with red
As away to the past his memory sped,
Upcalling the day of his great renown,
When he won and he wore the Scottish crown.
  Yet, come there shadow or come there shine,
  The spider is spinning his thread so fine.

"I have sat on the royal seat of Scone,"
  He muttered, below his breath;
"It's a luckless change—from a kingly throne
  To a felon's shameful death."
And he clenched his hand in his despair,
And he struck at the shapes that were gathering there,
Pacing his cell in impatient rage,
As a new-caught lion paces his cage.
  But, come there shadow or come there shine,
  The spider is spinning his web so fine.

"Oh, were it my fate to yield up my life
    At the head of my liegemen all,—
In the foremost shock of the battle-strife
    Breaking my country's thrall,
I'd welcome death from the foeman's steel,
Breathing a prayer for old Scotland's weal;
But here, where no pitying heart is nigh,
By a loathsome hand-it is hard to die."
    Yet, come there shadow or come there shine,
    The spider is spinning his thread so fine.

"Time and again have I fronted the pride
    Of the tyrant's vast array,
But only to see, on the crimson tide,
    My hopes swept far away.
Now a landless chief and a crownless king,
On the broad, broad earth not a living thing
To keep me court, save yon insect small,
Striving to reach from wall to wall."
    For, come there shadow or come there shine,
    The spider is spinning his thread so fine.

"Work, work as a fool, as I have done,
    To the loss of your time and pain—
The space is too wide to be bridged across,
    You but waste your strength in vain."
And Bruce, for the moment, forgot his grief,
His soul now filled with the same belief—
That, howsoever the issue went,
For evil or good was the omen sent.
    And, come there shadow or come there shine,
    The spider is spinning his thread so fine.

As a gambler watches his turning card
    On which his all is staked—
As a mother waits for the hopeful word

For which her soul has ached—
It was thus Bruce watched, with every sense
Centered alone in that look intense;
All rigid he stood, with unuttered breath,
Now white, now red, but still as death.
　　Yet, come there shadow or come there shine,
　　The spider is spinning his thread so fine.

　　Six several times the creature tried,
　　　　When at the seventh—"See! see!
　　He has spanned it over!" the captive cried,
　　　　"Lo! a bridge of hope to me;
Thee, God, I thank, for this lesson here
Has tutored my soul to PERSEVERE!"
And it served him well, for ere long he wore
In freedom the Scottish crown once more.
　　And, come there shadow or come there shine,
　　The spider is spinning his thread so fine.

JOHN BROUGHAM.

KATIE LEE AND WILLIE GREY.

　　Two brown heads with tossing curls,
　　Red lips shutting over pearls,
　　Bare feet, white and wet with dew,
　　Two black eyes, and two eyes blue,
　　Little girl and boy were they,
　　Katie Lee and Willie Grey.

　　They were standing where a brook,
　　Bending like a shepherd's crook,
　　Flashed its silver, and thick ranks
　　Of willow fringed its mossy banks—
　　Half in thought and half in play,
　　Katie Lee and Willie Grey.

They had cheeks like cherries red;
He was taller—'most a head.
She with arms like wreaths of snow,
Swung a basket to and fro
As she loitered, half in-play,
Chattering to Willie Grey.

"Pretty Katie," Willie said—
And there came a dash of red
Through the brownness of his cheek—
"Boys are strong and girls are weak,
And I'll carry, so I will,
Katie's basket up the hill."

Katie answered, with a laugh,
"You shall carry only half;"
And then tossing back her curls,
"Boys are weak as well as girls."
Do you think that Katie guessed
Half the wisdom she possessed?

Men are only boys grown tall;
Hearts don't change much after all;
And when, long years from that day,
Katie Lee and Willie Grey
Stood again beside the brook
Bending like a shepherd's crook—

Is it strange that Willie said,
While again a dash of red
Crossed the brownness of his cheek,
"I am strong and you are weak;
Life is but a slippery steep,
Hung with shadows cold and deep.

"Will you trust me, Katie dear—
Walk beside me without fear?

May I carry, if I will,
All your burdens up the hill?"
And she answered, with a laugh,
"No, but you may carry half."

Close beside the little brook,
Bending like a shepherd's crook,
Washing with its silver hands
Late and early at the sands,
Is a cottage, where to-day
Katie lives with Willie Grey.

In a porch she sits, and lo!
Swings a basket to and fro—
Vastly different from the one
That she swung in years agone,
This is long and deep and wide,
And has—*rockers at the side.*

J. H. PIXLEY.

TAKING MRS. JONES' CENSUS.

When the census enumerator knocked on Jones' door, it was opened by a fierce-looking woman with red hair. When he had explained his errand, she said, savagely:

"I sha'n't tell you a thing, you impudent vagabond!"

"But, madam, the Government——"

"It's none of the Government's business who lives here!"

"But the Government, madam, wants the names so that it can send to each person a splendid chromo, which——"

"What kind of chromos?" she asked. "Those with a blue girl putting green sunflowers around a pink sheep's neck, while a yellow cow looks through a mud-colored fence?"

"Yes," said the enumerator, "and with a glorious red sunset over behind the barn."

"Well, we have twenty-two of those chromos in the house now. Got 'em as prizes at the tea store, and we don't want any more. So you can quit!"

"Very well, madam; then I shall have to get the facts as well as I can. I will put you down as having eighteen children, nine boys and nine girls, and six of them twins, with red hair. How will that do?" asked the enumerator, making a memorandum with his pencil.

"Put down what you please. Only the twins and red hair are lies, and if you put them into the census report, Mr. Jones will sue you for libel."

"Ah! Jones is the name, is it? Let me see, I'll put you down as a Presbyterian, and Mr. Jones as a Baptist. How will that do?"

"My folks have been Methodists for centuries. As for the Joneses, you can class them among the sinners; put 'em under the head of Total Depravity, even if they are Episcopalians."

"May I ask what is Mr. Jones' occupation?"

"He is mostly occupied in going to picnics and to horse-races just now, spending the money that ought to buy me clothes."

"Has he no regular business?"

"No; 'tis irregular. He hasn't made a whole boot for a month."

"Shoemaker," said the enumerator to himself. "I am getting along. And now, madam, how old are you?"

"Who told you to ask?"

"The President. Gave special orders. Said on no account was I to quit until I got your exact age."

"Well, he'll find it out, drat his impudence, when I choose to tell him, and that's not yet."

"Suppose I say sixty-seven," suggested the enumerator, thoughtfully.

"You call me sixty-seven if you dare! I'm not an hour over forty-two, and I can prove it out of the family Bible. But it's nobody's business but mine how old I am. Jones is fifty-two, but nobody would believe it who knew him. A child has more sense."

"The next question is, 'What color are the various members of your family—white, black, mulatto, Chinese, or Indian?'"

"That," said Mrs. Jones, "is sheer insolence. We are all just as white as you are."

"No Chinese?"

"Certainly not."

"No Indians?"

"You daren't ask such a question if I had the kitchen poker with me."

"No colored people about?"

"Jimmy!" shouted Mrs. Jones; "bring me a kettle of hot water!"

"We will pass that, then," said the enumerator. "Now let me know how many of the family are blind, deaf, dumb, idiotic, insane, crippled, bed-ridden, paralyzed, feeble-minded, one-legged, dyspeptic, suffering from torpid livers, or hydrocephalus, or otherwise disabled?"

"Is that on the paper there?"

"Yes, ma'am."

"Well, it's outrageous! But there is nothing the matter with any of us, excepting that Jones is a little deaf in the right ear, and Tommy squints, and I always have lumbago in the fall, when Jones' chills come on. And Lucy has warts. Does the paper ask about warts?"

"I think not. The Government seems to be indifferent about the number of warts in the country."

"I wonder it don't want to know about 'em. I wonder it don't want to know how often I give Johnny paregoric and sugar for the stomach-ache. That'd be no worse than some of the things it does ask. What business is it of the President whether Mr. Jones has one leg or eleven? The number of Mr. Jones' legs has nothing to do with the prosperity of the country, has it? Well, then, it is scandalous to send you here to ask about 'em."

"Let me see," said the enumerator, running over his paper with the point of his lead pencil; "how many times have you been married? And mention, if you please, why it was that your husband, or husbands, expressed a preference for a homely woman with warm hair?"

The enumerator was a brave man, but he was small. Mrs. Jones, on the contrary, was large and muscular. When she let go of his collar, and he had collected his senses, he found himself lying in the geranium bed, covered with mud, and with his memorandum-book on the other side of the fence.

Mrs. Jones had retreated to the house, and double locked the door, while she went to the stable yard to unchain the dog.

The enumerator picked himself up and emerged from the front gate just in time to miss the dog. Then he went over to Smiley's, across the way, and, after obtaining a description of the Smiley family, Mrs. Smiley gave him a full account of Mrs. Jones' household, with a variety of picturesque, but not very flattering, information respecting Mrs. Jones' personal peculiarities.

When the enumerator hands in his description of the Joneses, he is going to make it mighty interesting for the general reader.   MAX ADELER.

THE LORD OF BURLEIGH.

In her ear he whispers gayly—
  "If my heart by signs can tell,
Maiden, I have watched thee daily,
  And I think thou lov'st me well."
She replies, in accents fainter—
  "There is none I love like thee."
He is but a landscape painter,
  And a village maiden she.
He to lips that fondly falter,
  Presses his, without reproof;
Leads her to the village altar,
  And they leave her father's roof.
"I can make no marriage present;
  Little can I give my wife;
Love will make our cottage pleasant,
  And I love thee more than life."

They, by parks and lodges going,
  See the lordly castles stand;
Summer woods, about them blowing,
  Made a murmur in the land.
From deep thought himself he rouses,
  Says to her that loves him well—
"Let us see these handsome houses,
  Where the wealthy nobles dwell."
So she goes, by him attended,
  Hears him lovingly converse,
Sees whatever fair and splendid
  Lay betwixt his home and hers;
Parks with oak and chestnut shady,
  Parks and ordered gardens great;
Ancient homes of lord and lady,
  Built for pleasure and for state.

All he shows her makes him dearer;
    Evermore she seems to gaze
On that cottage, growing nearer,
    Where they twain will spend their days.
Oh, but she will love him truly;
    He shall have a cheerful home;
She will order all things duly,
    When beneath his roof they come.
Thus her heart rejoices greatly,
    Till a gate-way she discerns,
With armorial bearings stately,
    And beneath the gate she turns—
Sees a mansion more majestic
    Than all those she saw before;
Many a gallant gay domestic
    Bows before him at the door.

And they speak in gentle murmur,
    When they answer to his call,
While he treads with footsteps firmer,
    Leading on from hall to hall.
And, while now she wonders blindly,
    Nor the meaning can divine,
Proudly turns he round, and kindly—
    "All of this is mine and thine."
Here he lives in state and bounty,
    Lord of Burleigh, fair and free;
Not a lord in all the county
    Is so great a lord as he.
All at once the color flushes
    Her sweet face, from brow to chin;
As it were with shame she blushes,
    And her spirit changed within.

Then her countenance all over
    Pale again as death did prove;

But he clasped her like a lover,
  And he cheered her soul with love.
So she strove against her weakness,
  Though at times her spirit sank;
Shaped her heart, with woman's meekness,
  To all duties of her rank.
And a gentle consort made he,
  And her gentle mind was such,
That she grew a noble lady,
  And the people loved her much.

But a trouble weighed upon her,
  And perplexed her night and morn,
With the burden of an honor
  Unto which she was not born.
Faint she grew, and even fainter,
  As she murmured—"Oh, that he
Were once more that landscape painter,
  Which did win my heart from me!"
So she drooped and drooped before him,
  Fading slowly from his side;
Three fair children first she bore him,
  Then, before her time, she died.

Weeping, weeping, late and early,
  Walking up and pacing down,
Deeply mourned the Lord of Burleigh,
  Burleigh House, by Stamford town.
And he came to look upon her,
  And he looked at her and said—
"Bring the dress and put it on her,
  That she wore when she was wed."
Then her people, softly treading,
  Bore to earth her body dressed
In the dress that she was wed in,
  That her spirit might have rest.

                    ALFRED TENNYSON.

THE PILGRIMS.

Methinks I see it now, that one solitary, adventurous vessel. the Mayflower of a forlorn hope, freighted with the prospects of a future state, and bound across the unknown sea. I behold it pursuing, with a thousand misgivings, the uncertain, the tedious voyage. Suns rise and set, and weeks and months pass, and winter surprises them on the deep, but brings them not the sight of the wished-for shore. I see them now, scantily supplied with provisions, crowded almost to suffocation in their ill-stored prison, delayed by calms, pursuing a circuitous route; and now driven in fury before the raging tempest, on the high and giddy wave. The awful voice of the storm howls through the rigging; the laboring masts seem straining from their base, the dismal sound of the pumps is heard; the ship leaps, as it were, madly, from billow to billow; the ocean breaks, and settles with ingulfing floods over the floating deck, and beats with deadening, shivering weight, against the staggered vessel. I see them, escaped from those perils, pursuing their all but desperate undertaking, and landed, at last, after a few months' passage, on the ice-clad rocks of Plymouth—weak and weary from the voyage, poorly armed, scantily provisioned, without shelter, without means, surrounded by hostile tribes.

Shut, now, the volume of history, and tell me, on any principle of human probability, what shall be the fate of this handful of adventurers? Tell me, man of military science, in how many months were they all swept off by the thirty savage tribes enumerated within the early limits of New England? Tell me, politician, how long did this shadow of a colony, on which your conventions and treaties had not smiled, languish on the distant coast? Student of history, compare for me the baffled projects, the deserted settlements, the abandoned adventures, of other times, and find the parallel of this! Was it the winter's storm, beating upon the houseless heads of women and children? was it hard labor and spare meals? was it disease? was it the tomahawk? was it the deep malady of a blighted hope, a ruined enterprise, and a broken heart, aching, in its last moments, at the recollection of the loved and left, beyond the sea?—was it some or all of these united, that hurried this forsaken company to their melancholy fate? And is it possible that neither of these causes, that not all combined, were able to blast this bud of hope! Is it possible that from a beginning so feeble, so frail, so worthy, not so much of admiration as of pity, there has gone forth a progress so steady, a growth so wonderful, an expansion so ample, a reality so important, a promise, yet to be fulfilled, so glorious!   EDWARD EVERETT.

THE FIELD OF WATERLOO.

Stop! for thy tread is an empire's dust;
    And earthquake's spoil is sepulchered below!
Is the spot marked with no colossal bust?
    Nor column trophied for triumphal show?
    None; but the moral's truth tells simpler so.
As the ground was before, thus let it be.
    How that red rain hath made the harvest grow!
And is this all the world has gained by thee,
Thou first and last of fields, king-making Victory?

There was a sound of revelry by night,
    And Belgium's capital had gathered then
Her beauty and her chivalry; and bright
    The lamps shone o'er fair women and brave men;
    A thousand hearts beat happily; and when
Music arose, with its voluptuous swell,
    Soft eyes looked love to eyes which spake again;
And all went merry as a marriage-bell.
But hush! hark! a deep sound strikes like a rising knell!

Did ye not hear it?   No; 'twas but the wind,
  Or the car rattling o'er the stony street;
On with the dance! let joy be unconfined!
  No sleep till morn, when youth and pleasure meet
  To chase the glowing hours with flying feet!——
But hark! that heavy sound breaks in once more,
  As if the clouds its echo would repeat;
And nearer, clearer, deadlier than before.
Arm! Arm! it is, it is the cannon's opening roar!

Within a windowed niche of that high hall
  Sat Brunswick's fated chieftain; he did hear
That sound the first amidst the festival,
  And caught its tone with death's prophetic ear;
  And when they smiled because he deemed it near
His heart more truly knew that peal too well,
  Which stretched his father on a bloody bier,
And roused the vengeance blood alone could quell;
He rushed into the field, and, foremost fighting, fell!

Ah! then and there was hurrying to and fro,
  And gathering tears, and tremblings of distress,
And cheeks all pale, which but an hour ago
  Blushed at the praise of their own loveliness;
  And there was sudden parting, such as press
The life from out young hearts, and choking sighs
  Which ne'er might be repeated; who could guess
If ever more should meet those mutual eyes,
Since upon night so sweet such awful morn could rise!

And there was mounting in hot haste; the steed,
  The mustering squadron, and the clattering car,
Went pouring forward with impetuous speed,
  And swiftly forming in the ranks of war;
  And the deep thunder, peal on peal, afar,
And near, the beat of the alarming drum ·

Roused up the soldier ere the morning star;
While thronged the citizens, with terror dumb,
Or whispering, with white lips, "The foe! they come!
    they come!"

Last noon beheld them full of lusty life;
  Last eve, in beauty's circle, proudly gay;
The midnight brought the signal-sound of strife
  The morn, the marshaling in arms—the day,
  Battle's magnificently stern array!
The thunder clouds close o'er it; which, when rent,
  The earth is covered thick with other clay,
Which her own clay shall cover, heaped and pent,
Rider and horse, friend, foe, in one red burial blent.

BYRON.

THE PAUPER'S DEATH-BED.

Tread softly—bow the head;
  In reverent silence bow;
No passing bell doth toll,
Yet an immortal soul
  Is passing now.

Stranger! however great,
  With lowly reverence bow;
There's one in that poor shed,
One by that paltry bed,
  Greater than thou.

Beneath that beggar's roof,
  Lo! Death doth keep his state;
Enter—no crowds attend;
Enter—no guards defend
  This palace gate.

That pavement, damp and cold,
　No smiling courtiers tread;
One silent woman stands,
Lifting with meager hands
　A dying head.

No mingling voices sound—
　An infant wail alone;
A sob suppressed—again
That short, deep gasp, and then
　The parting groan.

Oh! change!—Oh! wondrous change!
　Burst are the prison bars—
This moment there, so low,
So agonized, and now
　Beyond the stars!

Oh! change—stupendous change!
　There lies the soulless clod!
The sun eternal breaks—
The new immortal wakes—
　Wakes with his God!

CAROLINE BOWLES SOUTHEY.

THE DYING SOLDIER.

"Chaplain, I am dying, dying;
　Cut a lock from off my hair,
For my darling mother, chaplain,
　After I am dead, to wear;
Mind you, 'tis for mother, chaplain,
　She whose early teachings now
Soothe and comfort the poor soldier,
　With the death-dew on his brow!

"Kneel down, now, beside me, chaplain,
  And return my thanks to Him
Who so good a mother gave me,
  Oh, my eyes are growing dim!
Tell her, chaplain, should you see her,
  All at last with me was well;
Through the valley of the shadow
  I have gone, with Christ to dwell!

"Do not weep, I pray you, chaplain;
  Yes, ah! weep for mother dear;
I'm the only living son, sir,
  Of a widowed mourner here;
Mother! I am going, going
  To the land where angels dwell;
I commend you unto Jesus;
  Mother darling—fare you well!"

Downward from their thrones of beauty
  Looked the stars upon his face;
Upward on the wings of duty
  Sped the angel of God's grace.
Bearing through the heavenly portal,
  To his blessed home above,
The dead soldier's soul immortal,
  To partake of Christ's sweet love.

*   *   *   *   *   *   *

Far away, in humble cottage,
  Sits his mother, sad and lone;
And her eyes are red with weeping,
  Thinking of her absent son.
Suddenly Death's pallid presence
  Cast a shadow o'er her brow;
Smiling a sweet smile of welcome,
  She is with her loved ones now!

RICHARD COE.

A LOST MOTHER-IN-LAW.

A Pittsburgh paper the other day published an account of a corpse, which was shipped to that place on a railroad, but, which missed the connections somehow, two or three times, and didn't turn up for about a month.   It is a very odd coincidence that Dr. Robinson, of our village, had almost a precisely similar experience a month or two ago. He received a telegram from New York, from a person unknown to him, saying that his mother-in-law was dead, and that the body would be sent right on.   He waited for several days, and as the old lady failed to arrive, he made some inquiry about her at the express office.

The express people stirred around, and after a while ascertained that the remains had been sent through to Washington, and delivered by some blunder to Secretary Tracy, under the impression that the box contained the model of a new-fangled gunboat.

Dr. Robinson instantly telegraphed on to the secretary that if he didn't return the body promptly, he would have him arrested for embezzling his mother-in-law.   The next day he received an answer, saying that the box had been re-shipped, and stating that if he tried to palm any more of his old cadavers off on the national administration, he would be seized and shot.

But still the package didn't turn up, and the doctor again put the express people on the scent.   They discovered that it had somehow got off onto the Northern Central Railroad, and was lying in the office at Harrisburgh. They ordered it to be sent on.   It was coming all right on the next train, when the express car was attacked by masked robbers, who ran the coffin out, opened it, and then left in disgust.   Next morning the body was found standing against a tree, and the coroner wouldn't let it go until he had held an inquest on it, and collected his fees.

But finally it was re-shipped at York, Pa., and it appeared to be on the way home when a collision occurred, and the folks who came to the rescue concluded that this must be one of the killed. So another coroner sat on it, and then it was buried. The doctor compelled the express company to have it disinterred, and it was set in motion again.

It arrived at Wilmington on the Fourth of July, and the express messenger was so anxious to get away to view the fire-works, that he didn't push the box all the way into the car, and while the train was going over a creek, the car received a jolt, the box slid out and into the creek, and the unconscious old lady sailed down with the tide, and never made land until she reached the Delaware Breakwater, down opposite Cape May.

The doctor was perfectly wild about it, for nobody could tell where the box had got to. The people at the breakwater thought it must have fallen overboard from a steamer, and they telegraphed pretty nearly all over the world about it. At last the news reached the papers, and the express company investigated the matter, and had the body shipped toward home. Word was sent to the doctor that she was coming at last upon a certain train, so he got the funeral procession ready and marched it down to the depot to receive his deceased relative. When the train reached the station it went past without stopping, and the doctor was furious.

He telegraphed over to Wilmington, and got a promise that the box would be sent on the next train in about four hours. So the mourners all waited around in the sweltering heat, and sure enough, after a while, the box arrived. It was shot out at the station. They put it in the hearse and took it to the cemetery, where it was safely interred. Then the doctor felt easy at last, and he went home with a

rather light heart. When he entered the house he saw a
woman sitting in the parlor toasting her toes by the grate.
She turned around as he entered, and to his amazement
and horror he perceived that it was his mother-in-law.
His first impulse was to slam the door and run. But he
summoned up courage enough to say:

"Great Heaven! what are you doing here? How did
you ever come to and climb out of that sepulcher?"

She was inclined to behave ugly at first at receiving such
a greeting, but when the doctor explained the matter, she
agreed that it was the most extraordinary thing she ever
heard of. So the doctor started right out for the cemetery, and ordered the man to disinter those remains. In
about two hours the man called to say that he had dug
down about forty feet, and, strange to say, couldn't find
the body. Then the doctor felt cold creep all over him,
and he began to doubt if the old lady up stairs was real
flesh and blood after all. But he proceeded to the grave-
yard to examine the matter for himself, and to his relief he
found that the fool of a man had dug in the wrong place.
So they got the body up at last, and took a look at it, and
the doctor saw at once that there was a mistake. It was
not his mother-in-law at all.

While he was wondering what on earth it meant, he
heard that the Episcopal minister was rushing around trying to find out something about *his* dead and strayed
mother-in-law. His name was Rev. Dr. Robertson, and
Dr. Robinson gave him a look at the body in the box. It
was the minister's relative. Then the other doctor wanted
him to shoulder all those coroner's fees and funeral expenses, which the minister declined to do, on the ground
that the job had been unnecessarily botched, and so the
case was taken into court, and set down for trial at the
next term. We are awaiting the result with some anxiety.
Dr. Robinson says that if he is going to have other people's dead mothers-in-law shoved off on him by the law of

the land, he intends to emigrate, and reside permanently
somewhere else.   MAX ADELER.

TUBAL CAIN.

Old Tubal Cain was a man of might
  In the days when the earth was young,
By the fierce red light of his furnace bright,
  The strokes of his hammer rung;
And he lifted high his brawny hand
  On the iron glowing clear,
Till the sparks rushed out in scarlet showers
  As he fashioned the sword and spear.
And he sang, "Hurrah for my handiwork!
  Hurrah for the spear and sword!
Hurrah for the hand that shall wield them well!
  For he shall be king and lord."

To Tubal Cain came many a one,
  As he wrought by his roaring fire,
And each one prayed for a strong steel blade,
  As the crown of his desire;
And he made them weapons sharp and strong,
  Till they shouted loud in glee,
And gave him gifts of pearls and gold,
  And spoils of forest free.
And they sang, "Hurrah for Tubal Cain,
  Who hath given us strength anew!
Hurrah for the smith! hurrah for the fire!
  And hurrah for the metal true!"

But a sudden change came o'er his heart
  Ere the setting of the sun,
And Tubal Cain was filled with pain
  For the evil he had done.

He saw that men, with rage and hate,
　　Made war upon their kind;
That the land was red with the blood they shed
　　In their lust for carnage blind.
And he said, "Alas, that ever I made,
　　Or that skill of mine should plan,
The spear and the sword, for men whose joy
　　Is to slay their fellow-man!"

And for many a day old Tubal Cain
　　Sat brooding o'er his woe;
And his hand forbore to smite the ore,
　　And his furnace smoldered low;
But he rose at last with a cheerful face,
　　And a bright, courageous eye,
And bared his strong right arm for work,
　　While the quick flames mounted high;
And he sang, "Hurrah for my handiwork!"
　　And the red sparks lit the air—
"Not alone for the blade was the bright steel made"—
　　And he fashioned the first plowshare.

And men, taught wisdom from the past,
　　In friendship joined their hands,
Hung the sword in the hall, the spear on the wall,
　　And plowed the willing lands;
And sang, "Hurrah for Tubal Cain!
　　Our stanch good friend is he;
And, for the plowshare and the plow,
　　To him our praise shall be.
But while oppression lifts its head,
　　Or a tyrant would be lord,
Though we may thank him for the plow,
　　We'll not forget the sword."

　　　　　　　　　　CHARLES MACKAY.

THE HOUR OF DEATH.

Leaves have their time to fall,
And flowers to wither at the north wind's breath
And stars to set—but all,
Thou hast all seasons for thine own, oh Death!

Day is for mortal care,
Eve for glad meetings round the joyous hearth,
Night for the dreams of sleep, the voice of prayer—
But all for Thee, thou mightiest of the earth.

The banquet hath its hour,
Its feverish hour of mirth, and song, and wine;
There comes a day for grief's o'erwhelming power,
A time for softer tears—but all are thine.

Youth and the opening rose
May look like things too glorious for decay,
And smile at thee—but thou are not of those
That wait the ripened bloom to seize their prey.

Leaves have their time to fall,
And flowers to wither at the north wind's breath,
And stars to set—but all,
Thou hast all seasons for thine own, oh Death!

We know when moons shall wane,
When summer-birds from far shall cross the sea,
When autumn's hue shall tinge the golden grain—
But who shall teach us when to look for thee?

Is it when Spring's first gale
Comes forth to whisper where the violets lie?
Is it when roses in our paths grow pale?—
They have *one* season—*all* are ours to die!

Thou art where billows foam,
Thou art where music melts upon the air;
Thou art around us in our peaceful home,
And the world calls us forth—and thou art there.

Thou art where friend meets friend,
Beneath the shadow of the elm to rest—
Thou art where foe meets foe, and trumpets rend
The skies, and swords beat down the princely crest.

Leaves have their time to fall,
And flowers to wither at the north wind's breath,
And stars to set—but all,
Thou hast all seasons for thine own, oh Death!

FELICIA HEMANS.

THE HOUSEKEEPER'S SOLILOQUY.

Here's a big washing to be done—
One pair of hands to do it—
Sheets, shirts and stockings, coats and pants,
How will I e'er get through it?

Dinner to get for six or more,
No loaf left o'er from Sunday;
And baby cross as he can live—
He's always so on Monday.

'Tis time the meat was in the pot,
The bread was worked for baking,
The clothes were taken from the boil—
Oh, dear! the baby's waking!

Hush, baby dear! there, hush-sh-sh!
I wish he'd sleep a little,

'Till I could run and get some wood,
　To hurry up the kettle.

Oh, dear! oh, dear! if P—— comes home,
　And finds things in this pother,
He'll just begin to tell me all
　About his tidy mother!

How nice her kitchen used to be,
　Her dinner always ready
Exactly when the noon-bell rang—
　Hush, hush, dear little Freddy!

And then will come some hasty words,
　Right out before I'm thinking—
They say that hasty words from wives
　Set sober men to drinking.

Now, is not that a great idea,
　That men should take to sinning,
Because a weary, half-sick wife,
　Can't always smile so winning?

When I was young, I used to earn
　My living without trouble,
Had clothes, and pocket money, too,
　And hours of leisure double.

I never dreamed of such a fate,
　When I, a-lass! was courted—
Wife, mother, nurse, seamstress, cook, housekeeper,
chambermaid, laundress, dairy woman, and scrub gener-
ally, doing the work of six,
　For the sake of being supported!

MRS. F. D. GAGE.

THE TRAITOR'S DEATH-BED.

Fifty years ago, in a rude garret, near the loneliest sub-
urbs of the city of London, lay a dying man. He was but
half dressed, though his legs were concealed in long military boots. An aged minister stood beside the rough
couch. The form was that of a strong man, grown old
through care more than age. There was a face that you
might look upon once, and yet wear it in your memory
forever.

Let us bend over the bed, and look upon that face. A
bold forehead seamed by one deep wrinkle, visible between the brows—long locks of dark hair, sprinkled with
gray; lips firmly set, yet quivering, as though they had a
life separate from the life of the man; and then, two large
eyes—vivid, burning, unnatural in their steady glare. Ay,
there was something terrible in that face—something so
full of unnatural loneliness—unspeakable despair, that the
aged minister started back in horror. But look! those
strong arms are clutching at the vacant air; the death-
sweat stands in drops on that bold brow—the man is dying. Throb—throb—throb—beats the death-watch in the
shattered wall. "Would you die in the faith of the Christian?" faltered the preacher, as he knelt there on the damp
floor.

The white lips of the death-stricken man trembled, but
made no sound. Then, with the strong agony of death
upon him, he rose into a sitting posture. For the first time
he spoke. "Christian!" he echoed, in that deep tone which
thrilled the preacher to the heart; "will that faith give me
back my honor? Come with me, old man, come with me,
far over the waters. Ha! we are there! This is my native
town. Yonder is the church in which I knelt in childhood;
yonder the green on which I sported when a boy. But an-

other flag waves yonder, in place of the flag that waved when I was a child.

"And listen, old man, were I to pass along the streets, as I passed when but a child, the very babes in their cradles would raise their tiny hands, and curse me! The graves in yonder church-yard would shrink from my footsteps; and yonder flag would rain a baptism of blood upon my head!"

That was an awful death-bed. The minister had watched "the last night" with a hundred convicts in their cells, but had never beheld a scene so terrible as this. Suddenly the dying man arose; he tottered along the floor. With those white fingers, whose nails were blue with the death-chill, he threw open a valise. He drew from thence a faded coat of blue, faced with silver, and the wreck of a battle-flag.

"Look ye, priest! this faded coat is spotted with my blood!" he cried, as old memories seemed stirring at his heart. "This coat I wore, when I first heard the news of Lexington; this coat I wore, when I planted the banner of the stars on Ticonderoga! that bullet-hole was pierced in the fight of Quebec; and now, I am a—let me whisper it in your ear!" He hissed that single burning word into the minister's ear. "Now, help me, priest! help me to put on this coat of blue; for you see"—and a ghastly smile came over his face—"there is no one here to wipe the cold drops from my brow; no wife, no child. I must meet Death alone; but I will meet him, as I have met him in battle, without a fear!"

And, while he stood arraying his limbs in that worm-eaten coat of blue and silver, the good minister spoke to him of faith in Jesus. Yes, of that great faith, which pierces the clouds of human guilt, and rolls them back from the face of God. "Faith!" echoed the strange man, who stood there, erect, with the death-chill on his brow; "Faith! Can it give me back my honor? Look ye, priest!

there, over the waves, sits George Washington, telling to his comrades the pleasant story of the eight years' war; there, in his royal halls, sits George of England, bewailing, in his idiotic voice, the loss of his colonies! And here am I!—I, who was the first to raise the flag of freedom, the first to strike a blow against that king—here am I, dying! oh, dying like a dog!"

The awe-stricken preacher started back from the look of the dying man, while throb—throb—throb—beats the death-watch, in the shattered wall. "Hush! silence along the lines there!" he muttered, in that wild, absent tone, as though speaking to the dead; "silence along the lines! not a word—not a word, on peril of your lives! Hark you. Montgomery! we will meet in the center of the town—we will meet there in victory, or die!—Hist! silence, my men, not a whisper, as we move up those steep rocks! Now on, my boys, now on! Men of the wilderness, we will gain the town! Now, up with the banner of the stars—up with the flag of freedom, though the night is dark, and the snow falls! Now! now, one more blow, and Quebec is ours!"

And look! his eye grows glassy. With that word on his lips, he stands there—ah! what a hideous picture of despair; erect, livid, ghastly; there for a moment, and then he falls—he is dead! Ah, look at that proud form, thrown cold and stiff upon the damp floor. In that glassy eye there lingers, even yet, a horrible energy—a sublimity of despair.

Who is this strange man lying there alone, in this rude garret; this man, who, in all his crimes, still treasured up in that blue uniform, that faded flag? Who is this being of horrible remorse—this man, whose memories seem to link something with heaven, and more with hell?

Let us look at that parchment and flag. The aged minister unrolls that faded flag; it is a blue banner gleaming with thirteen stars. He unrolls that parchment; it is a

colonel's commission in the Continental Army, addressed
to BENEDICT ARNOLD. And there, in that rude hut, while
the death-watch throbbed like a heart in the shattered wall;
there, unknown, unwept, in all the bitterness of desola-
tion, lay the corpse of the patriot and the traitor.

GEORGE LIPPARD.

THE BRAVE AT HOME.

The maid who binds her warrior's sash,
  With smile that well her pain dissembles,
The while beneath her drooping lash
  One starry tear-drop hangs and trembles.
Though Heaven alone records the tear,
  And fame shall never know the story,
Her heart has shed a drop as dear
  As e'er bedewed the field of glory.

The wife who girds her husband's sword,
  'Mid little ones who weep or wonder,
And bravely speaks the cheering word,
  What though her heart be rent asunder,
Doomed nightly in her dreams to hear
  The bolts of death around him rattle,
Had shed as sacred blood as e'er
  Was poured upon a field of battle!

The mother who conceals her grief,
  While to her breast her son she presses,
Then breathes a few brave words and brief,
  Kissing the patriot brow she blesses,
With no one but her secret God
  To know the pain that weighs upon her,
Sheds holy blood as e'er the sod
  Received on Freedom's field of honor!

T. BUCHANAN READ.

PSALM OF MARRIAGE.

Tell me not in idle jingle,
  "Marriage is an empty dream!"
For the girl is dead that's single,
  And girls are not what they seem.

Life is real! Life is earnest!
  Single blessedness a fib!
"Man thou art, to man returnest!"
  Has been spoken of the rib.

Not enjoyment, and not sorrow,
  Is our destined end or way;
But to act that each to-morrow
  Finds us nearer marriage day.

Life is long, and youth is fleeting,
  And our hearts, though light and gay,
Still like pleasant drums are beating
  Wedding marches all the way.

In the world's broad field of battle,
  In the bivouac of life,
Be not like dumb driven cattle!
  Be a heroine—a wife!——

Trust no future, howe'er pleasant,
  Let the dead past bury its dead!
Act—act to the living Present!
  Hearts within and hope ahead!

Lives of married folks remind us
  We can live our lives as well,
And, departing, leave behind us,
  Such examples as shall "tell."

Such examples that another,
　Wasting time in idle sport,
A forlorn, unmarried brother,
　Seeing, shall take heart and court.

Let us, then, be up and doing,
　With a heart on triumph set,
Still contriving, still pursuing,
　And each one a husband get.

　　　　　　　　　　PHŒBE CARY.

THE WATER MILL.

Oh! listen to the water mill, through all the live-long
　　day,
As the clicking of the wheel wears hour by hour away;
How languidly the autumn wind doth stir the withered
　　leaves,
As on the field the reapers sing, while binding up the
　　sheaves,
A solemn proverb strikes my mind, and as a spell is cast,
"The mill will never grind with water that is past."

Soft summer winds revive no more leaves strewn o'er earth
　　and main,
The sickle never more will reap the yellow garnered
　　grain,
The rippling stream flows ever on, aye tranquil, deep and
　　still,
But never glideth back again to busy water mill,
The solemn proverb speaks to all, with meaning deep and
　　vast,
"The mill will never grind with water that is past."

Oh! clasp the proverb to thy soul, dear loving heart and
　　true,

For golden years are fleeting by, and youth is passing
too,
Ah! learn to make the most of life, nor lose one happy
day,
For time will ne'er return sweet joys, neglected, thrown
away,
Nor leave one tender word unsaid—true love alone will
last—
"The mill will never grind with water that is past."

Oh! the wasted hours of life, that have swiftly drifted by,
Alas! the good we might have done, all gone without a
sigh,
Love that we might once have saved by a single kindly
word,
Thoughts conceived but ne'er expressed, perishing, un-
penned, unheard—
Oh! take the lesson to thy soul, forever clasp it fast—
"The mill will never grind with water that is past."

Work on while yet the sun doth shine, thou man of
strength and will,
The streamlet ne'er doth useless glide by clicking water
mill,
Nor wait until to-morrow's light beams brightly on the
way,
For all that thou canst call thine own lies in the phrase,
to-day—
Possessions, power and blooming health, must all be lost
at last—
"The mill will never grind with water that is past."

Oh! love thy God and fellow man, thyself considered
last,
For come it will when thou must scan dark errors of the
past,

Soon will this fight of life be o'er, and earth recede from
    view,
And heaven in all its glory-shine, where all is pure and
    true,
Ah! then thou'lt see more clearly still, the proverb deep
    and vast,
"The mill will never grind with water that is past."

D. C. McCallum.

THE OLD ACTOR'S STORY.

Mine is a wild, strange story—the strangest you ever
    heard;
There are many who won't believe it, but it's gospel, every
    word;
It's the biggest drama of any in a long, adventurous life;
The scene was a ship, and the actors—were myself and my
    new-wed wife.

You musn't mind if I ramble, and lose the thread now and
    then;
I'm old, you know, and I wander—it's a way with old
    women and men,
For their lives lie all behind them, and their thoughts go
    far away,
And are tempted afield, like children lost on a summer
    day.

The years must be five-and-twenty that have passed since
    that awful night,
But I see it again this evening, I can never shut out the
    sight.
We were only a few weeks married, I and the wife, you
    know,
When we had an offer for Melbourne, and made up our
    minds to go.

We'd acted together in England, traveling up and down
With a strolling band of players, going from town to
town;
We played the lovers together—we were leading lady and
gent—
And at last we played in earnest, and straight to the church
we went.

The parson gave us his blessing, and I gave Nellie the
ring,
And swore that I'd love and cherish, and endow her with
everything.
How we smiled at that part of the service when I said, "I
thee endow!"
But as to the "love and cherish," I meant to keep that
vow.

We were only a couple of strollers; we had coin when the
show was good,
When it wasn't we went without it, and we did the best we
could.
We were happy, and loved each other, and laughed at the
shifts we made—
Where love makes plenty of sunshine, there poverty casts
no shade.

Well, at last we got to London, and did pretty well for a
bit;
Then the business dropped to nothing, and the manager
took a flit—
Stepped off one Sunday morning, forgetting the treasury
call;
But our luck was in, and we managed right on our feet to
fall.

We got an offer for Melbourne—got it that very week.

Those were the days when thousands went over to fortune seek,
The days of the great gold fever, and a manager thought
the spot
Good for a "spec," and took us as actors among his lot.

We hadn't a friend in England—we'd only ourselves to
please—
And we jumped at the chance of trying our fortune across
the seas.
We went on a sailing vessel, and the journey was long and
rough;
We hadn't been out a fortnight before we had had enough.

But use is a second nature, and we'd got not to mind a
storm,
When misery came upon us— came in a hideous form.
My poor little wife fell ailing, grew worse, and at last so
bad
That the doctor said she was dying—I thought 'twould
have sent me mad—

Dying where leagues of billows seemed to shriek for their
prey,
And the nearest land was hundreds—ay, thousands—of
miles away.
She raved one night in a fever, and the next lay still as
death,
So still I'd to bend and listen for the faintest sign of
breath.

She seemed in a sleep, and sleeping, with a smile on her
thin, wan face,
She passed away one morning, while I prayed to the
throne of grace.
I knelt in the little cabin, and prayer after prayer I said,

Till the surgeon came and told me it was useless—my wife
    was dead!

Dead! I wouldn't believe it. They forced me away that
    night,
For I raved in my wild despairing, the shock sent me mad
    outright.
I was shut in the farthest cabin, and I beat my head on
    the side,
And all day long in my madness, "They've murdered her!"
    I cried.

They locked me away from my fellows—put me in cruel
    chains,
It seems I had seized a weapon to beat out the surgeon's
    brains.
I cried in my wild, mad fury, that he was a devil sent
To gloat o'er the frenzied anguish with which my heart
    was rent.

I spent that night with the irons heavy upon my wrists,
And my wife lay dead quite near me. I beat with my
    fettered fists.
Beat at my prison panels, and then—O God!—and then
I heard the shrieks of women, and the tramp of hurrying
    men.

I heard the cry, "Ship a-fire!" caught up by a hundred
    throats,
And over the roar the captain shouting to lower the boats;
Then cry upon cry, and curses, and the crackle of burning
    wood,
And the place grew hot as a furnace, I could feel it where
    I stood.

I beat at the door and shouted, but never a sound came
    back,

And the timbers above me started, till right through a
    yawning crack
I could see the flames shoot upward, seizing on mast and
    sail,
Fanned in their burning fury by the breath of the howl-
    ing gale.

I dashed at the door in fury, shrieking, "I will not die!
Die in this burning prison!"—but I caught no answering
    cry.
Then, suddenly, right upon me, the flames crept up with
    a roar,
And their fiery tongues shot forward, cracking my prison
    door.

I was free—with the heavy iron door dragging me down to
    death;
I fought my way to the cabin, choked with the burning
    breath
Of the flames that danced around me like man-mocking
    fiends at play.
And then—O God! I can see it, and shall to my dying
    day.

There lay my Nell as they'd left her, dead in her berth
    that night;
The flames flung a smile on her features—a horrible, lurid
    light.
God knows how I reached and touched her, but found my-
    self by her side;
I thought she was living a moment, I forgot that my Nell
    had died.

In the shock of those awful seconds reason came back to
    my brain;
I heard a sound as of breathing, and then a low cry of
    pain;

Oh, was there mercy in heaven? Was there a God in the
    skies?
The dead woman's lips were moving, the dead woman
    opened her eyes.

I cursed like a madman raving—I cried to her, "Nell! my
    Nell!"
They had left us alone and helpless, alone in that burning
    hell;
They had left us alone to perish—forgotten me living—
    and she
Had been left for the fire to bear her to heaven, instead of
    the sea.

I clutched at her, roused her shrieking, the stupor was on
    her still;
I seized her in spite of my fetters—fear gave a giant's will.
God knows how I did it, but blindly I fought through the
    flames and the wreck
Up—up to the air, and brought her safe to the untouched
    deck.

We'd a moment of life together—a moment of life, the
    time
For one last word to each other—'twas a moment supreme,
    sublime.
From the trance we'd for death mistaken, the heat had
    brought her to life,
And I was fettered and helpless, so we lay there, husband
    and wife!

It was but a moment, but ages seemed to have passed
    away,
When a shout came over the water, and I looked, and lo,
    there lay,
Right away from the vessel, a boat that was standing by;

They had seen our forms on the vessel, as the flames lit
    up the sky.

I shouted a prayer to Heaven, then called to my wife, and
    she
Tore with new strength at my fetters—God helped her,
    and I was free;
Then over the burning bulwarks we leaped for one chance
    of life.
Did they save us?   Well, here I am, sir, and yonder's my
    dear old wife.

We were out in the boat till daylight, when a great ship
    passing by
Took us on board, and at Melbourne landed us by and by.
We've played many parts in dramas since we went on that
    famous trip,
But ne'er such a scene together as we had on the burning
    ship!

GEORGE R. SIMS.

THE CANE-BOTTOMED CHAIR.

In tattered old slippers that toast at the bars,
And a ragged old jacket perfumed with cigars,
Away from the world and its toils and its cares,
I've a snug little kingdom up four pair of stairs.

To mount to this realm is a toil, to be sure,
But the fire there is bright and the air rather pure;
And the view I behold on a sunshiny day
Is grand through the chimney-pots over the way.

This snug little chamber is cramm'd in all nooks
With worthless old knickknacks and silly old books,

And foolish old odds and foolish old ends,
Crack'd bargains from brokers, cheap keepsakes from
    friends.

Old armor, prints, pictures, pipes, china (all crack'd),
Old rickety tables, and chairs broken-backed;
A twopenny treasury, wondrous to see;
What matter? 'tis pleasant to you, friend, and me.

No better divan need the sultan require
Than the creaking old sofa that basks by the fire;
And 'tis wonderful, surely, what music you get
From the rickety, ramshackle, wheezy spinet.

That praying-rug came from a Turcoman's camp;
By Tiber once twinkled that brazen old lamp;
A Mameluke fierce yonder dagger has drawn;
'Tis a murderous knife to toast muffins upon.

Long, long through the hours, and the night, and the
    chimes,
Here we talk of old books, and old friends, and old times;
As we sit in a fog made of rich Latakie
This chamber is pleasant to you, friend, and me.

But of all the cheap treasures that garnish my nest,
There's one that I love and cherish the best;
For the finest of couches that's padded with hair
I never would change thee, my cane-bottomed chair.

'Tis a bandy-legg'd, high-shoulder'd, worm-eaten seat,
With a creaking old back, and twisted old feet;
But since the fair morning when Fanny sat there,
I bless thee and love thee, old cane-bottomed chair.

If chairs have but feeling, in holding such charms,
A thrill must have passed through your withered old arms!
I looked, and I longed, and I wished in despair;
I wished myself turned to a cane-bottomed chair.

It was but a moment she sat in this place,
She'd a scarf on her neck, and a smile on her face!
A smile on her face, and a rose in her hair,
And she sat there, and bloomed in my cane-bottomed
    chair.

And so I have valued my chair ever since,
Like the shrine of a saint, or the throne of a prince;
Saint Fanny, my patroness sweet I declare,
The queen of my heart and my cane-bottomed chair.

When the candles burn low, and the company's gone,
In the silence of night as I sit here alone—
I sit here alone, but we yet are a pair—
My Fanny I see in my cane-bottomed chair.

She comes from the past and revisits my room;
She looks as she then did, all beauty and bloom;
So smiling and tender, so fresh and so fair,
And yonder she sits in my cane-bottomed chair.

WM. M. THACKERAY.

THE CLOWN'S BABY.

It was on a western frontier;
    The miners, rugged and brown,
Were gathered around the posters;
    The circus had come to town!
The great tent shone in the darkness
    Like a wonderful palace of light,
And rough men crowded the entrance—
    Shows didn't come every night!

Not a woman's face among them;
    Many a face that was bad,
And some that were only vacant,
    And some that were very sad.

And behind a canvas curtain,
　　In a corner of the place,
The clown, with chalk and vermilion,
　　Was "making up" his face.

A weary-looking woman,
　　With a smile that still was sweet,
Sewed on a little garment,
　　With a cradle at her feet.
Pantaloon stood ready and waiting;
　　It was time for the going on,
But the clown in vain searched wildly;
　　The "property-baby" was gone!

He murmured, impatiently hunting,
　　"It's strange, I cannot find—
There! I've looked in every corner;
　　It must have been left behind!"
The miners were stamping and shouting,
　　They were not patient men.
The clown bends over the cradle—
　　"I must take *you*, little Ben!"

The mother started and shivered,
　　But trouble and want were near;
She lifted her baby gently;
　　"You'll be *very* careful, dear?"
"Careful? You foolish darling"—
　　How tenderly it was said!
What a smile shone through the chalk and paint —
　　"I love each hair of his head!"

The noise rose into an uproar,
　　Misrule for a time was king;
The clown, with a foolish chuckle,
　　Bolted into the ring.

But as, with a squeak and flourish,
  The fiddles closed their tune,
"You'll hold him as if he was made of glass?"
  Said the clown to Pantaloon.

The jovial fellow nodded;
  " I've a couple myself," he said,
"I know how to handle 'em, bless you!
  Old fellow, go ahead!"
The fun grew fast and furious,
  And not one of all the crowd
Had guessed that the baby was alive,
  When he suddenly laughed aloud.

Oh, that baby-laugh! It was echoed
  From the benches with a ring,
And the roughest customer there sprang up
  With, "Boys, it's the real thing!"
The ring was jammed in a minute,
  Not a man that did not strive
For "a shot at holding the baby,"
  The baby that was "alive!"

He was thronged by kneeling suitors,
  In the midst of the dusty ring,
And he held his court right royally—
  The fair little baby king—
Till one of the shouting courtiers,
  A man with a bold, hard face,
The talk, for miles, of the country,
  And the terror of the place,

Raised the little king to his shoulder,
  And chuckled, "Look at that!"
As the chubby fingers clutched his hair,
  Then, "Boys, hand round the hat!"

There never was such a hatful
  Of silver, and gold, and notes;
People are not always penniless
  Because they don't wear coats!

And then, "Three cheers for the baby!"
  I tell you, those cheers were meant,
And the way in which they were given
  Was enough to raise the tent.
And then there was sudden silence,
  And a gruff old miner said,
"Come, boys, enough of this rumpus!
  It's time it was put to bed."

So, looking a little sheepish,
  But with faces strangely bright,
The audience, somewhat lingeringly,
  Flocked out into the night.
And the bold-faced leader chuckled—
  "He wasn't a bit afraid!
He's as game as he is good-looking;
  Boys, that was a show that *paid!*"

                        MARGARET VANDEGRIFT.

SOME TIME.

Last night, my darling, as you slept,
  I thought I heard you sigh,
And to your little crib I crept
  And watched a space thereby;
Then, bending down, I kissed your brow—
  For, oh, I love you so—
You are too young to know it now,
  But some time you shall know.

Some time, when, in a darkened place
  Where others come to weep,

Your eyes shall see a weary face
   Calm in eternal sleep.
The speechless lips, the wrinkled **brow,**
   The patient smile may show—
You are too young to know it now,
   But some time you shall know.

Look backward, then, into the years,
   And see me here to-night—
See, oh, my darling! how my tears
   Are falling as I write;
And feel once more upon your brow
   The kiss of long ago—'
You are too young to know it now,
   But some time you shall know.

EUGENE FIELD.

A FREE SEAT.

He was old and poor and a stranger
   In the great metropolis,
As he bent his steps thitherward
   To a stately edifice;
Outside he inquires, "What church is this?"
   "Church of Christ," he hears them say;
"Ah! just the place I am looking for;
   I trust he is in here to-day."

He passed through the spacious columned door
   And up the carpeted aisle,
And as he passed, on many a face
   He saw surprise and a smile.
From pew to pew, up one entire side,
   Then across the broad front space;
From pew to pew, down the other side
   He walked with the same slow pace.

Not a friendly voice had bid him sit
   To list to the gospel truth,
Not a sign of deference had been paid
   To the aged one by youth.
No door was opened by generous hand,
   The pews were paid for—rented,
And he was a stranger, old and poor,
   Not a heart to him relented.

And as he paused outside a moment to think,
   Then passed into the street,
Up to his shoulder he lifted a stone
   That lay in the dust at his feet.
And bore it up the broad, grand aisle,
   In front of the ranks of pews,
Choosing a place to see and hear,
   He made a seat for his use.

Calmly sitting upon the huge stone,
   Folding his hands on his knees,
Slowly, reviewing the worshipers,
   A great confusion he sees.
Many a cheek crimsoned with shame,
   Some whisper together sore,
And wished they had been more courteous
   To a stranger, old and poor.

As if by magic some fifty doors
   Opened simultaneously,
And as many seats and books and hands
   Are proffered hastily;
Changing his stone for a crimsoned pew
   And wiping a tear away,
He thinks it was a mistake, after all,
   And that Christ came late that day.

The preacher's discourse was eloquent,
　The organ in finest tone,
But the most impressive sermon heard
　Was preached by an humble stone.
'Twas a lesson of lowliness and worth
　That lodged in many a heart,
And that church preserves that sacred stone,
　That the truth may not depart.

ANONYMOUS.

ST. LEON'S TOAST.

The feast is o'er!　Now brimming wine
In lordly cup is seen to shine
　Before each eager guest;
And silence fills the crowded hall,
As deep as when the herald's call
　Thrills in the loyal breast.

Then up arose the noble host,
Who smiling cried, "A toast! a toast!
　To all our ladies fair!
Here, before all, I pledge the name
Of Staunton's proud and beauteous dame—
　The Lady Gundamere!"

Quick to his feet each gallant sprang,
And joyous was the shout that rang,
　As Stanley gave the word;
And every cup was raised on high,
Nor ceased the loud and gladsome cry,
　Till Stanley's voice was heard.

"Enough, enough," he smiling said,
And lowly bent his haughty head;

"That all may have their due,
Now each in turn must play his part,
And pledge the lady of his heart,
   Like gallant knight and true!"

Then one by one each guest stood up,
And drained in turn the brimming cup,
   And named the loved one's name;
And each, as hand on high he raised,
His lady's grace and beauty praised,
   Her constancy and fame.

'Tis now St. Leon's turn to rise;
On him are fixed those countless eyes—
   A gallant knight is he;
Envied by some, admired by all,
Far-famed in lady's bower and hall—
   The flower of chivalry.

St. Leon raised his kindling eye,
And held the sparkling cup on high;
   "I drink to one," he said,
"Whose image never may depart,
Deep graven on this grateful heart,
   Till memory be dead.

"To one whose love for me shall last,
When lighter passions long have past,
   So holy 'tis and true;
To one whose love hath longer dwelt,
More deeply fixed, more keenly felt,
   Than any pledged by you."

Each guest upstarted at the word,
And laid a hand upon his sword,
   With fury-flashing eye;

And Stanley said, "We crave the name,
Proud knight, of this most peerless dame,
   Whose fame you count so high."

St. Leon paused, as if he would
Not breathe her name in careless mood
   Thus lightly to another;
Then bent his noble head, as though
To give that word the reverence due,
   And gently said, "My mother!"

                    WALTER SCOTT.

THE JINERS.

She was about forty-five years old, well dressed, had black hair, rather thin and tinged with gray, and eyes in which gleamed the fires of determination not easily balked. She walked into the mayor's office and requested a private interview, and having obtained it, and satisfied herself that the law students were not listening at the keyhole, said slowly, solemnly, and impressively:

"I want a divorce."

"What for? I supposed you had one of the best of husbands," said the mayor.

"I s'pose that's what everybody thinks; but if they knew what I've suffered in ten years, they'd wonder I hadn't scalded him long ago. I ought to, but for the sake of the young ones I've borne it, and said nothing. I've told him, though, what he might depend on, and now the time's come; I won't stand it, young ones or no young ones. I'll have a divorce, and if the neighbors want to blab themselves hoarse about it they can, for I won't stand it another day."

"But what's the matter? Doesn't your husband provide for you? Doesn't he treat you kindly?" pursued the mayor.

"We get victuals enough, and I don't know but he's as true and kind as men in general, and he's never knocked any of us down, I wish he had; then I'd get him into jail, and know where he was of nights," retorted the woman.

"Then what is your complaint against him?"

"Well, if you must know, he's one of them plaguey jiners."

"A what?"

"A jiner—one of them pesky fools that's always jining something. There can't nothing come along that's dark and sly and hidden, but he jines it. If anybody should get up a society to burn his house down, he'd jine it just as soon as he could get in; and if he had to pay for it he'd go all the suddener. We hadn't been married more'n two months before he jined the Know Nothin's. We lived on a farm then, and every Saturday night he'd come tearing in before supper, grab a fistful of nut cakes, and go off gnawing them, and that's the last I'd see of him till morning. And every other night he'd roll and tumble in his bed, and holler in his sleep, 'Put none but Americans on guard—George Washington;' and rainy days he would go out in the corn-barn, and jab at a picture of King George with an old bagnet that was there. I ought to put my foot down then, but he fooled me so with his lies that I let him go and encouraged him in it.

"Then he jined the Masons. P'raps you know what them be, but I don't, 'cept they think they are of the same kind of critters that built Solomon's temple; and of all the nonsense and gab about worshipful master, and square and compasses, and sich like that we had in the house for the next six months, you never see the beat. And he's never outgrowed it nuther. What do you think of a man, squire, that'll dress himself in a white apron, about big enough for a monkey's bib, and go marching up and down and making motions, and talking foolish lingo at the picture of George Washington, in a green jacket and an apron covered over with eyes and columns and other queer pictures! Ain't he a loonytick? Well, that's my Sam, and I've stood it as long as I am goin' to.

"The next lunge the old fool made was into the Odd Fellows. I made it warm for him when he came home and told me he'd jined them, but he kinder pacified me by telling me they had a sort of branch show that took in women, and he'd get me in as soon as he found how to do it. Well, one night he come home and said I'd been proposed, and somebody had blackballed me. Did it himself, of course. Didn't want me around knowing about his goings on. Of course he didn't, and I told him so.

"Then he jined the Sons of Malter. Didn't say nothing to me about it, but sneaked off one night, pretendin' he'd go to sit up with a sick Odd Fellow, and I never found it out, only he come home looking like a man who had been through a threshing machine, and I wouldn't do a thing for him until he owned up. And so it's gone from bad to wus, jinin' this and that and t'other, till he's worship minister of the Masons, and goodness of hope of the Odd Fellows, and sword swallower of the Finnegans, and virgin cerus of the Grange, and grand mogul of the Sons of Indclence, and two-edged tomahawk of the United Order of Red Men, and tale bearer of the Merciful Manikins, and skipper of the Guild Caratrine Columbus, and grand oriental bouncer of the Royal Arcaners, and big wizard of the Arabian Nights. and pledge passer of the Reform Club, and chief bugler of the Irish Mechanics, and purse-keeper of the Order of Canadian Conscience, and double-barreled dictator of the Knights of the Brass Circles, and standard-bearer of the Royal Archangels, and sublime porte of the Onion League, and chief butler of

the Celestial Cherubs, and puissant potentate of the Petri-
fied Pollywogs, and goodness only knows what else. I've
borne it and borne it, hopin' he'd get 'em all jined after a
while, but 'tain't no use, and when he'd got into a new
one, and been made grand guide of the Nights of Horror,
I told him I'd quit, and I will."

Here the mayor interrupted, saying:

"Well, your husband is pretty well initiated, that's a
fact; but the court will hardly call that a good cause for
divorce. The most of the societies you mention are com-
posed of honorable men with excellent reputations. Many
of them, though called lodges, are relief associations and
mutual insurance companies, which, if your husband
should die, would take care of you, and would not see you
suffer if you were sick."

"See me suffer when I'm sick! Take care of me when
he's dead! Well, I guess not; I can take care of myself
when he's dead; and if I can't I can get another! There's
plenty of 'em! And they needn't bother themselves when
I am sick either. If I want to be sick and suffer, it's none
of their business, especially after all the suffering I've had
when I ain't sick, because of their carryin's on. And
you needn't try to make me believe it's all right, either.
I know what it is to live with a man that jines so many
lodges that he don't never lodge at home."

"Oh, that's harmless amusement," quietly remarked the
mayor; "and if all that you say about your husband is
really as you affirm, it affords strong proof that he must be
a man endowed with an unusual amount of earnestness of
purpose, as well as a large degree of popularity."

She looked him square in the eyes and said:

"I believe you are a jiner yourself."

He admitted that he was to a certain extent, and she
arose and said:

"I would not have thought it. A man like you, chairman of a Sabbath-school—it's enough to make a woman

take pizen! But I don't want anything of you. I want a lawyer that don't belong to nobody or nothin'." And she bolted out of the office to hunt up a man that wasn't a jiner.   ANONYMOUS.

THE CHARITY DINNER.

Time: Half-past six o'clock. Place: The London Tavern. Occasion: Fifteenth Annual Festival of the Society for the Distribution of Blankets and Top-Boots among the Natives of the Cannibal Islands.

On entering the room, we find more than two hundred noblemen and gentlemen already assembled; and the number is increasing every minute. The preparations are now complete, and we are in readiness to receive the chairman. After a short pause, a little door at the end of the room opens, and the great man appears, attended by an admiring circle of stewards and toadies, carrying white wands like a parcel of charity schoolboys bent on beating the bounds. He advances smilingly to his post at the principal table, amid deafening and long-continued cheers.

The dinner now makes its appearance, and we yield up ourselves to the enjoyments of eating and drinking. These important duties finished, and grace having been beautifully sung by the vocalists, the real business of the evening commences. The usual loyal toasts having been given, the noble chairman rises, and, after passing his fingers through his hair, he places his thumbs in the armholes of his waistcoat, gives a short preparatory cough, accompanied by a vacant stare around the room, and commences as follows:

"MY LORDS AND GENTLEMEN:—It is with feelings of mingled pleasure and regret that I appear before you this evening; of pleasure, to find that this excellent and world-wide-known society is in so promising a condition; and of regret that you have not chosen a worthier chairman, in fact, one who is more capable than myself of dealing with a subject of such vital importance as this. (Loud cheers.) But, although I may be unworthy of the honor, I am proud to state that I have been a subscriber to this society from its commencement; feeling sure that nothing can tend more to the advancement of civilization, social reform, fire-side comfort, and domestic economy among the Cannibals, than the diffusion of blankets and top-boots. (Tremendous cheering, which lasts for several minutes.) Here, in this England of ours, which is an island surrounded by water, as I suppose you all know—or, as our great poet so truthfully and beautifully expresses the same fact, 'England bound in by the triumphant sea'—what, down the long vista of years, have conduced more to our successes in arms, and arts, and song, than blankets? Indeed, I never gaze upon a blanket without my thoughts reverting fondly to the days of my early childhood. Where should we all have been now but for those warm and fleecy coverings? My Lords and Gentlemen! Our first and tender memories are all associated with blankets; blankets when in our nurses' arms, blankets in our cradles, blankets in our cribs, blankets to our French bedsteads in our school-days, and blankets to our marital four-posters now. Therefore, I say, it becomes our bounden duty as men— and, with feelings of pride, I add, as Englishmen—to initiate the untutored savage, the wild and somewhat uncultivated denizen of the prairie into the comfort and warmth of blankets; and to supply him, as far as practicable, with those reasonable, seasonable, luxurious, and useful appendages. At such a moment as this, the lines of another poet strike familiarly upon the ear. Let me see, they are something like this—ah—ah——

"Blankets have charms to soothe the savage breast,
" And to—to do—a——

I forget the rest. (Loud cheers.) Do we grudge our
money for such a purpose? I answer fearlessly, No!
Could we spend it better at home? I reply most emphatically, No! True, it may be said that there are thousands
of our own people who at this moment are wandering
about the streets of this great metropolis without food to
eat or rags to cover them. But what have *we* to do with
them? Our thoughts, our feelings, and our sympathies
are all wafted on the wings of charity to the dear and interesting Cannibals in the far-off islands of the great Pacific
Ocean. (Hear, hear.) Besides, have not our own poor
the work-houses to go to; the luxurious straw of the casual
wards to repose upon, if they please; mutton broth to
bathe in, and the ever toothsome, although somewhat scanty
allowance of 'toke' provided for them? If people choose to
be poor, is it our business? And let it ever be remembered that our own people are not savages and man-eaters;
and, therefore, our philanthropy would be wasted upon
them. (Overwhelming applause.) To return to our subject. Perhaps some person or persons here may wonder
why we should not send out side-springs and bluchers, as
well as top-boots. To those I will say, that top-boots
alone answer the object desired—namely, not only to keep
the feet dry, but the legs warm, and thus to combine the
double uses of shoes and stockings. Is it not an instance
of the remarkable foresight of this society, that it pur-
posely abstains from sending out any other than top-boots?
To show the gratitude of the Cannibals for the benefits
conferred upon them, I will just mention that, within the
last few weeks, his illustrious Majesty, Hokey Pokey Wan-
key Fum the First—surnamed by his loving subjects 'The
Magnificent,' from the fact of his wearing, on Sundays, a
shirt-collar and an eye-glass as full court costume—has
forwarded the president of the society a very handsome

present, consisting of two live alligators, a boa-constrictor, and three pots of preserved Indian, to be eaten with toast; and I am told by competent judges, that it is quite equal to Russian caviare.

"My Lords and Gentlemen—I will not trespass on your patience by making any further remarks; knowing how incompetent I am—no, no! I don t mean that—knowing how incompetent you all are—no! I don't mean that either —but you all know what I mean. Like the ancient Roman lawgiver, I am in a peculiar position; for the fact is, I cannot sit down—I mean to say, that I cannot sit down without saying that, if there ever was an institution, it is this institution; and, therefore, I beg to propose, 'Prosperity to the Society for the Distribution of Blankets and Top-Boots among the Natives of the Cannibal Islands.' "

The toast having been cordially responded to, his lordship calls upon Mr. Duffer, the secretary, to read the report. Whereupon that gentleman, who is of a bland and oily temperament, and whose eyes are concealed by a pair of green spectacles. produces the necessary document, and reads in the orthodox manner.

"Thirtieth Half-yearly Report of the Society for the Distribution of Blankets and Top-Boots to the Natives of the Cannibal Islands.

"The society having now reached its fifteenth anniversary, the committee of management beg to congratulate their friends and subscribers on the success that has been attained.

"When the society first commenced its labors, the generous and noble-minded natives of the islands, together with their king—a chief whose name is well-known in connection with one of the most sterling and heroic ballads of this country—attired themselves in the light but somewhat insufficient costume of their tribe—viz: little before, nothing behind, and no sleeves, with the occasional addition of a pair of spectacles; but now, thanks to this useful association, the upper classes of the Cannibals seldom appear in public without their bodies being enveloped in blankets, and their feet incased in top-boots.

"When the latter useful articles were first introduced into the islands, the society's agent had a vast amount of trouble to prevail upon the natives to apply them to their proper purpose; and, in their work of civilization, no less than twenty of its representatives were massacred, roasted, and eaten. But we persevered; we overcame the natural antipathy of the Cannibals to wear any covering to their feet; until, after a time, the natives discovered the warmth and utility of boots; and now they can scarcely be induced to remove them until they fall off through old age.

"During the past half-year, the society has distributed no less than 71 blankets, and 128 pairs of top-boots; and your committee, therefore, feel convinced that they will not be accused of inaction. But a great work is still before them; and they earnestly invite co-operation, in order that they may be enabled to supply the whole of the Cannibals with these comfortable, nutritious and savory articles.

"As the balance-sheet is rather a lengthy document, I will merely quote a few of the figures for your satisfaction. We have received, during the last half-year, in subscriptions, donations, and legacies, the sum of 5,403*l*. 6*s*. 3-4*d*. We have disbursed for advertising, etc., 222*l*. 6*s*. 2*d*. Rent, rates, and taxes, 305*l*. 10*s*. 1-4*d*. Seventy-one pairs of blankets, at 20*s*. per pair, have taken 71*l*. exactly; and and 128 pairs of top-boots, at 21*s*. per pair, cost 134*l*. some odd shillings. The salaries and expenses of the management amount to 1.307*l*. 4*s*. 2 1-2*d*.; and sundries, which include committee meetings and traveling expenses, have absorbed the remainder of the sum, and amount to 3,268*l*. 9*s*. 1 3-4*d*. So that we have expended on the dear and interesting Cannibals the sum of 205*l*., and the remainder of the sum—amounting to 5,198*l.*—has been devoted to the working expenses of the society."

The reading concluded, the secretary resumes his seat amid hearty applause, which continues until Mr. Alderman Gobbleton rises, and, in a somewhat lengthy and discursive speech, in which the phrases "the Corporation of the City of London, "suit and service," "ancient guild," "liberties and privileges," and "Court of Common Council," figure frequently, states that he agrees with everything the noble chairman has said; and has, moreover, never listened to a more comprehensive and exhaustive document than the one just read; which is calculated to satisfy even the most obtuse and hard-headed of individuals.

Gobbleton is a great man in the city. He has either been lord mayor, sheriff, or something of the sort; and, as a few words of his go a long way with his friends and admirers, his remarks are very favorably received.

"Clever man, Gobbleton!" says a common councilman, sitting near us, to his neighbor, a languid swell of the period.

"Ya-as, vewy! Wemarkable style of owatowy—gweat fluency," replies the other.

But attention, if you please, for M. Hector de Longuebeau, the great French writer, is on his legs. He is staying in England for a short time, to become acquainted with our manners and customs.

"MILORS AND GENTLEMANS!" commences the Frenchman, elevating his eyebrows and shrugging his shoulders.

"Milors and Gentlemans—You excellent chairman, M. le Baron de Mount-Stuart, he have say to me, 'Make de toast.' Den I say to him dat I have no toast to make; but he nudge my elbow ver soft, and say sat dere is von toast dat nobody but von Frenchman can make proper, and, derefore, wid your kind permission, I vill made de toast. 'De brevete is de sole of de feet,' as you great philoso-

phere, Dr. Johnson, do say in dat amusing little vork of
his, de Pronouncing Dictionnaire; and, derefore, I vill not
say ver moch to de point. Ven I vos a boy, about so moch
tall, and used for to promenade de streets of Marseilles et
of Rouen, vid no feet to put onto my shoe, I nevare to
have expose dat dis day vould to have arrive. I vos to begin de vorld as von garcon—or, vat you call in dis coun-
trie, von vaitaire in cafe—vere I vork ver hard, vid no
habillemens at all to put onto myself, and ver little food to
eat, excep' von old blue blouse vat vas give to me by de
proprietaire, just for to keep myself fit to be showed at;
but, tank goodness, tings dey have change ver moch·for
me since dat time, and I have rose myself, seulment par
mon industrie et perseverance. (Loud cheers.) Ah! mes
amis! ven I hear to myself de flowing speech, de oration
magnifique of you Lor' Maire, Monsieur Gobbledown, I
feel dat it is von great privilege for von stranger to sit at
de same table, and to eat de same food, as dat grand, dat
majestique man, who are de terreur of de voleurs and de
brigands of de metropolis; and who is also, I for to suppose, a halterman and de chef of you common scoundrel.
Milors and gentlemans, I feel dat I can perspire to no
greatare honneur dan to be von common scoundrelman
myself; but helas! dat plaisir are not for me, as I are not
freeman of your great cite, not von liveryman servant of
von of you compagnies joint-stock. But I must not forget de toast.   Milors and Gentlemans!   De immortal
Shakispeare he have write, 'De ting of beauty are de joy
for nevermore.' It is de ladies who are de toast. Vat is
more entrancing dan de charmante smile, de soft voice, de
vinking eye of de beautiful lady? It is de ladies who do
sweeten de cares of life. It is de ladies who are de guid-
ing stars of our existence. It is de ladies who do cheer
but not inebriate, and, derefore, vid all homage to dere
sex, de toast dat I have to propose is, 'De Ladies! God
bless dem all!' "

And the little Frenchman sits down amid a perfect tempest of cheers.

A few more toasts are given, the list of subscriptions is read, a vote of thanks is passed to the chairman, and the Fifteenth Annual Festival of the Society for the Distribution of Blankets and Top-Boots among the Natives of the Cannibal Islands is at an end.

LITCHFIELD MOSELY.

THE TWO GLASSES.

There sat two glasses, filled to the brim,
On a rich man's table, rim to rim;
One was ruddy and red as blood,
And one as clear as the crystal flood.

Said the glass of wine to the paler brother,
"Let us tell the tales of the past to each other;
I can tell of the banquet and revel and mirth,
And the proudest and grandest souls on earth
Fell under my touch as though struck by blight,
Where I was king, for I ruled in might.
From the heads of kings I have torn the crown;
From the heights of fame I have hurled men down.
I have blasted many an honored name,
I have taken virtue and given shame;
I have tempted the youth with a sip, to taste
That has made his future a barren waste.
Greater, far greater than king am I,
Or than any army beneath the sky.
I have made the arm of the driver fail,
And sent the train from the iron rail;
I have made good ships go down at sea,
And the shrieks of the lost were sweet to me,
For they said, 'Behold, how great you be!

Fame, strength, wealth, genius before you fall,
For your might and power are over all.'
Ho! ho! pale brother," laughed the wine,
"Can you boast of deeds as great as mine?"

Said the water glass, "I cannot boast
Of a king dethroned or a murdered host;
But I can tell of a heart once sad,
By my crystal drops made light and glad;
Of thirsts I've quenched, of brows I've laved,
Of hands I have cooled, and souls I have saved;
I have leaped through the valley, dashed down the moun-
    tain,
Flowed in the river and played in the fountain,
Slept in the sunshine and dropped from the sky,
And everywhere gladdened the landscape and eye.
I have eased the hot forehead of fever and pain,
I have made the parched meadows grow fertile with grain;
I can tell of the powerful wheel of the mill,
That ground out the flour and turned at my will;
I can tell of manhood debased by you,
That I have lifted and crowned anew.
I cheer, I help, I strengthen and aid,
I gladden the heart of the man and maid;
I set the chained wine-captive free,
And all are better for knowing me."

These are the tales they told each other,
The glass of wine and the pale brother,
As they sat together filled to the brim,
On the rich man's table, rim to rim.

                              ELLA WHEELER WILCOX.

THE SONG OF THE CAMP.

"Give us a song!" the soldier cried,
    The outer trenches guarding,
When the heated guns of the camps allied
    Grew weary of bombarding.

The dark Redan, in silent scoff,
    Lay grim and threat'ning under;
And the tawny mound of the Malakoff
    No longer belched its thunder.

There was a pause. A guardsman said:
    "We storm the forts to-morrow;
Sing while we may, another day
    Will bring enough of sorrow."

They lay along the battery's side,
    Below the smoking cannon;
Brave hearts from Severn and from Clyde,
    And from the banks of Shannon.

They sang of love, and not of fame,
    Forgot was Britain's glory;
Each heart recalled a different name,
    But all sang "Annie Laurie."

Voice after voice caught up the song,
    Until its tender passion
Rose like an anthem, rich and strong,
    Their battle eve confession.

Dear girl, her name he dared not speak,
    But as the song grew louder,
Something upon the soldier's cheek
    Washed off the stains of powder.

Beyond the dark'ning ocean burned
　　The bloody sunset's embers,
While the Crimean valleys learned
　　How English love remembers.

And once again a fire of hell
　　Rained on the Russian quarters,
With scream of shot and burst of shell
　　And billowing of the mortars.

And Irish Nora's eyes are dim
　　For a singer dumb and gory;
And English Mary mourns for him
　　Who sang of "Annie Laurie."

Sleep, soldiers! still in honored rest
　　Your truth and valor wearing;
The bravest are the tenderest,
　　The loving are the daring.

BAYARD TAYLOR.

TOM'S WIFE.

They sat at the club a-smoking
　　(Tom's wife was just then dead),
And Jack was talking of old times
　　And this is what he said:

"Have you ever loved a woman, Tom,
　　Whom you did not wish to wed—
Content to live in the sunshine
　　Her presence round you shed?
Could you see her wed another
　　And feel naught of regret,
But go on loving ever
　　Till the tide of life had set?

"I loved a woman once, Tom,
  'Tis some few years ago,
When love beat in my heart, Tom,
  With a glad, triumphant glow;
But I never told the love, Tom,
  That I'm telling now to you,
Though you know I could win a woman
  If I only cared to woo.

"But I hold there's a better love, Tom,
  Than the love that seeks to win—
A love that deems earth-marriage
  Almost a hateful sin;
You smile and shake your head, Tom,
  In your old, half-cynic way,
And you think my notion wild, Tom,
  So I've little more to say.

We've been chums many a day, Tom,
  And have had no cause for strife;
But the maid I loved with this love of mine
  Was the girl just dead—your wife."

W. H. HARRISON.

THE BIBLE.

There is a book, the treasure of a nation, which has now become the fable and the reproach of the world, though in former days the star of the East, to whose pages all the great poets of the western world have gone to drink in divine inspiration, and from which they have learned the secret of elevating our hearts, and transporting our souls with superhuman and mysterious harmonies. This book is the Bible—the Book of books. In it Dante saw his terrific visions; from it Petrarch learned to modulate the voice of his complainings; from that burning forge the poet of Sorrentum drew for the splendid brightness of his songs.

In the Bible are written the annals of heaven, of earth, and of the human race. In it, as in the divinity itself, is contained that which was, which is, and which is to come. In the first page is recorded the beginning of time and of all things—in its last, the end of all things and of time. It begins with Genesis, which is an idyl; it finishes with the Apocalypse of St. John, which is a funeral hymn.

Genesis is beautiful as the first breeze which refreshed the world, as the first flower which budded forth in the fields, as the first tender word which humanity pronounced, as the first sun that rose in the East. The Apocalypse is sad, like the last throb of nature, like the last ray of light, like the last glance of the dying; and between that funeral hymn and that idyl we behold all generations pass, one after another, before the sight of God, and one after another, all nations.

There all catastrophes are related or predicted, and, therefore, immortal models for all tragedies are to be found there. There we find the narration of all human griefs, and therefore, the Biblical harps resound mournfully, giving the tone to all lamentations and to all elegies. Who will again moan like Job, when, driven to the earth by the mighty hand that afflicted him, he fills with his groanings and waters with his tears the valleys of Idumea?

Who will again lament as Jeremiah lamented, wandering around Jerusalem, and abandoned of God and men? Who will be mournful and gloomy, with the gloom and mournfulness of Ezekiel, the poet of great woes and tremendous punishments, when he gave to the winds his impetuous inspiration, the terror of Babylon? Who shall again sing like Moses, when, after crossing the Red Sea, he chanted the victory of Jehovah, the defeat of Pharaoh, the liberty of his people?

Who shall again chant a hymn of victory like that which

was sung by Deborah, the Sibyl of Israel, the Amazon of the Hebrews, the strong women of the Bible? And if from hymns of victory you pass to hymns of praise, what temple shall ever resound like that of Israel, when those sweet harmonious voices arose to heaven, mingled with the soft perfume of the roses of Jericho, and with the aroma of oriental incense?

If you seek for models of lyric poetry, what lyre shall we find comparable to the harp of David, the friend of God, who listened to the sweet harmonies and caught the soft tones of the harps of angels, or to that of Solomen, the wisest and most fortunate of monarchs, the inspired writer of the Song of Songs; he who put his wisdom into sentences and proverbs, and finished by pronouncing that all was vanity?

If you seek for models of bucolic poetry, where will you find them so fresh and so pure as in the scriptural era of the patriarchate, when the woman and the fountain and the flower were friends, because they were all united— each one by itself the symbol of primitive simplicity and of candid innocence?

A prodigious book that, gentlemen, in which the human race began to read thirty three centuries ago, and although reading it every day, every night, and every hour, have not yet finished its perusal. A prodigious book that, in which all is computed, before the science of calculation was invented; in which, without the study of the languages, we are informed of the origin of languages; in which, without astronomical studies, the revolutions of the stars are computed; in which, without historical documents, we are instructed in history; in which, without physical studies, the laws of nature are revealed.

A prodigious book that, which sees all and knows all; which knows the thoughts that arise in the heart of man, and those which are present to the mind of God; which views that which passes in the abysses of the sea, and that

which takes place in the bosom of the earth; which re-
lates or predicts all the catastrophes of nations, and in
which are contained and heaped together all the treasures
of mercy, all the treasures of justice, and all the treasures
of vengeance.

A book, in short, gentlemen, which, when the heavens
shall fold together like a gigantic scroll, and the earth
shall faint away, and the sun withdraw its light, and the
stars grow pale, will remain alone with God, because it
is his eternal word, and shall resound eternally in the
heavens.   DONOSO CORTES.

THE BIVOUAC OF THE DEAD.

The muffled drum's sad roll has beat
    The soldier's last tattoo;
No more on life's parade shall meet
    That brave and fallen few.
On Fame's eternal camping-ground
    Their silent tents are spread,
And glory guards with solemn round
    The bivouac of the dead.
No rumor of the foe's advance
    Now swells upon the wind,
No troubled thought at midnight haunts
    Of loved ones left behind;
No vision of the morrow's strife
    The warrior's dream alarms,
No braying horn or screaming fife
    At dawn shall call to arms.
Their shivered swords are red with rust,
    Their plumed heads are bowed,
Their haughty banner trailed in dust
    Is now their martial shroud—
And plenteous funeral tears have washed

The red stains from each brow,
And the proud forms by battle gashed
Are free from anguish now.
The neighing troop, the flashing blade,
The bugle's stirring blast,
The charge, the dreadful cannonade,
The din and shout are passed—
Nor war's wild note, nor glory's peal,
Shall thrill with fierce delight
Those breasts that never more may feel
The rapture of the fight.
Like the fierce northern hurricane
That sweeps his great plateau,
Flushed with the triumph yet to gain
Came down the serried foe—
Who heard the thunder of the fray
Break o'er the field beneath,
Knew well the watchword of that day
Was victory or death.
Full many a mother's breath hath swept
O'er Angostura's plain,
And long the pitying sky has wept
Above its molder'd slain.
The raven's scream or eagle's flight,
Or shepherd's pensive lay,
Alone now wake each solemn height
That frowned o'er that dread fray.
Sons of the Dark and Bloody Ground,
Ye must not slumber there,
Where stranger steps and tongues resound
Along the heedless air!
Your own proud land's heroic soil
Shall be your fitter grave;
She claims from war its richest spoil—
The ashes of her brave.
Thus 'neath their parent turf they rest,

Far from the gory field,
  Borne to a Spartan mother's breast
    On many a bloody shield.
The sunshine of their native sky
    Shines sadly on them here,
And kindred eyes and hearts watch by
    The heroes' sepulcher.
Rest on, embalmed and sainted dead!
    Dear as the blood ye gave;
No impious footstep here shall tread
    The herbage of your grave!
Nor shall your glory be forgot
    While Fame her record keeps,
Or Honor points the hallowed spot
    Where Valor soundly sleeps.
Yon marble minstrel's voiceless stone
    In deathless song shall tell,
When many a vanished year hath flown,
    The story how ye fell;
Nor wreck, nor change, nor winter's blight,
    Nor time's remorseless doom,
Can dim one ray of holy light
    That gilds your glorious tomb.

THEODORE O'HARA.

THE NEEDLE.

The gay belle of fashion may boast of excelling
  In waltz or cotillon, at whist or quadrille;
And seek admiration by vauntingly telling
  Of drawing, and painting, and rustical skill;
But give me the fair one, in country or city,
  Whose home and its duties are dear to her heart,
Who cheerfully warbles some rustical ditty,
  While plying the needle with exquisite art;

The bright little needle—the swift-flying needle,
　The needle directed by beauty and art.

If love have a potent, a magical token, .
　A talisman, ever resistless and true—
A charm that is never evaded or broken,
　A witchery certain the heart to subdue.
'Tis this—and his armory never has furnished
　So keen and unerring, or polished a dart;
Let beauty direct it, so pointed and burnished,
　And, oh! it is certain of touching the heart.
The bright little needle—the swift-flying needle,
　The needle directed by beauty and art.

Be wise, then, ye maidens, nor seek admiration
　By dressing for conquest, and flirting with all;
You *never*, whate'er be your fortune or station,
　Appear half so lovely at rout or at ball,
As gayly convened at a work-covered table,
　Each cheerfully active and playing her part,
Beguiling the task with a song or a fable,
　And plying the needle with exquisite art;
The bright little needle—the swift-flying needle,
　The needle directed by beauty and art.

SAMUEL WOODWORTH.

THE GAMBLER'S WIFE.

Dark is the night! how dark!—no light! no fire!
Cold on the hearth the last faint sparks expire!
Shivering she watches by the cradle side
For him who pledged her love—last year a bride!
"Hark! 'tis his footstep! No—'tis past; 'tis gone;
Tick!—tick! How wearily the time crawls on.
Why should he leave me thus? He once was kind,
And I believed 'twould last—how mad! how blind!

Rest thee, my babe—rest on!· 'Tis hunger's cry!
Sleep, for there is no food, the fount is dry.
Famine and cold their wearying work have done;
My heart must break! And thou!"— The clock strikes
  one.
"Hush! 'tis the dice-box. Yes, he's there, he's there!
For this, for this, he leaves me to despair!
Leaves love, leaves truth, his wife, his child—for what?
The wanton's smile—the villain—and the sot!
Yet I'll not curse him; no—'tis all in vain.
'Tis long to wait, but sure he'll come again;
And I could starve and bless him, but for you,
My child—*his* child—oh, fiend!"—The clock strikes two.
"Hark! how the sign-board creaks, the blast howls by!
Moan—moan! A dirge swells through the cloudy sky!
Ha! 'tis his knock—he comes—he comes once more—
'Tis but the lattice flaps. Thy hope is o'er.
Can he desert me thus? He knows I stay
Night after night in loneliness to pray
For his return—and yet he sees no tear.
No, no! it cannot be. He will be here.
Nestle more closely, dear one, to my heart;
Thou'rt cold—thou'rt freezing; but we will not part.
Husband, I die! Father, it is not he!
Oh, Heaven, protect my child!"—The clock strikes three.
They're gone! they're gone! The glimmering spark hath
  fled,
The wife and child are number'd with the dead!
On the cold earth, outstretched in solemn rest,
The child lies frozen on its mother's breast!
The gambler came at last—but all was o'er—
Dead silence reigned around—he groaned—he spoke no
  more!

E. R. COATES.

THE BATTLE OF FONTENOY.

At Fontenoy, Belgium, on May 11, 1745, the French Army under Marshal Saxe, was opposed by the allied troops of the English, Dutch, and Austrians. The allied forces were commanded by the Duke of Cumberland, and fought so valiantly that they had already gained the hill, the possession of which assured a decisive victory, when Marshal Saxe, determined upon a last and almost hopeless effort, called up his reserves, among which was the brigade of Irish exiles. Pointing to the English, Marshal Saxe said to Lord Clare, who was in command of the Irish Brigade, *"There are your Saxon foes!"* In a minute the exclamation passed from lip to lip, and the Irish exiles fought so desperately that the opposing forces, after a long and fierce fight, were driven from the field, with a loss of 8.000 killed, wounded, and prisoners. The loss of the French was about the same, showing that the conflict had been well contested on both sides, and had been decided by the valor and determination of the very men of whom George the Second said, "Cursed be the laws which deprive me of such subjects!"

Thrice, at the heights of Fontenoy, the English column
    failed,
And twice the lines of Saint Antoine the Dutch in vain
    assailed;
For town and slope were filled with fort and flanking bat-
    tery,
And well they swept the English ranks, and Dutch auxil-
    iary.
As vainly through De Barri's wood the British soldiers
    burst,
The French artillery drove them back, diminished and dis-
    persed.
The bloody Duke of Cumberland beheld with anxious
    eye,
And ordered up his last reserve, his latest chance to try.
On Fontenoy, on Fontenoy, how fast his generals ride!
And mustering come his chosen troops, like clouds at
    eventide.

Six thousand English veterans in stately column tread,

Their cannon blaze in front and flank, Lord Hay is at their
　　head;
Steady they step adown the slope—steady they climb the
　　hill;
Steady they load—steady they fire, moving right onward
　　still,
Betwixt the wood and Fontenoy, as through a furnace
　　blast,
Through rampart, trench, and palisade, and bullets show-
　　ering fast;
And, on the open space above, they rose, and kept their
　　course,
With ready fire and grim resolve, that mocked at hostile
　　force.
Past Fontenoy, past Fontenoy, while thinner grow their
　　ranks—
They break, as broke the Zuyder Zee through Holland's
　　ocean banks!

More idly than the summer flies, French tirailleurs rush
　　round.
As stubble to the lava tide, French squadrons strew the
　　ground;
Bomb-shell, and grape, and round-shot tore, still on they
　　marched and fired—
Fast from each volley grenadier and voltigeur retired.
"Push on, my household cavalry!" King Louis madly
　　cried;
To death they rush, but rude their shock—not unavenged
　　they died.
On through the camp the column trod—King Louis turns
　　his rein.
"Not yet, my liege," Saxe interposed, "the Irish troops
　　remain!"
And Fontenoy, famed Fontenoy, had been a Waterloo—
Were not these exiles ready then, fresh, vehement, and true?

"Lord Clare," he says, "you have your wish, *there are
your Saxon foes!*"
The marshal almost smiles to see, so furiously he goes!
How fierce the look these exiles wear, who're wont to be
so gay,
The treasured wrongs of fifty years are in their hearts to-
day—
The treaty broken, ere the ink wherewith 'twas writ could
dry,
Their plundered homes, their ruined shrines, their women's
parting cry,
Their priesthood hunted down like wolves, their country
overthrown—
Each looks as if revenge for all was staked on him alone.
On Fontenoy, on Fontenoy, nor ever yet elsewhere
Rushed on to fight a nobler band than these proud exiles
were.

O'Brien's voice is hoarse with joy, as, halting, he com-
mands,
"Fix bayonets! Charge! Like mountain storm rush on
these fiery bands!"
Thin is the English column now, and faint their volleys
grow,
Yet must'ring all the strength they have, they make a gal-
lant show.
They dress their ranks upon the hill to face that battle-
wind—
Their bayonets the breakers' foam; like rocks the men be-
hind!
One volley crashes from the line, when through the surg-
ing smoke,
With empty guns clutched in their hands, the headlong
Irish broke.
On Fontenoy, on Fontenoy, hark to that fierce huzza!
"Revenge! remember Limerick! dash down the Sassenach!"

Like lions leaping at a fold, when mad with hunger's
    pang,
Right up against the English line the Irish exiles sprang;
Bright was their steel—'tis bloody now; their guns are
    filled with gore;
Through shattered ranks, and severed files, and trampled
    flags they tore;
The English strove with desperate strength, paused, ral-
    lied, staggered, fled—
The green hill-side is matted close with dying and with
    dead.
Across the plain, and far away, passed on that hideous
    wrack,
While cavalier and fantassin dash in upon their track.
On Fontenoy, on Fontenoy, like eagles in the sun,
With bloody plumes the Irish stand—the field is fought
    and won!

THOMAS DAVIS.

THE DRONES OF THE COMMUNITY.

    Those gilded flies
That, basking in the sunshine of a Court,
Fatten on its corruption—what are they?
The drones of the community! they feed
On the mechanic's labor; the starved hind
For them compels the stubborn glebe to yield
Its unshared harvests; and yon squalid form,
Leaner than fleshless misery, that wastes
A sunless life in the unwholesome mine
Drags out in labor a protracted death,
To glut *their* grandeur. Many faint with toil,
That few may know the cares and woe of sloth.
Whence, think'st thou, kings and parasites arose?
Whence that unnatural line of drones, who heap

Toil and unvanquishable penury
On those who build their palaces, and bring
Their daily bread?—From vice, black, loathsome vice;
From rapine, madness, treachery, and wrong;
From all that genders misery, and makes
Of earth this thorny wilderness; from lust
Revenge, and murder—And, when Reason's voice,
Loud as the voice of nature, shall have waked
The Nations; and mankind perceive that vice
Is discord, war, and misery—that virtue
Is peace, and happiness, and harmony;
When man's maturer nature shall disdain
The playthings of its childhood—kingly glare
Will lose its power to dazzle; its authority
Will silently pass by; the gorgeous throne
Shall stand unnoticed in the regal hall,
Fast falling to decay, whilst falsehood's trade
Shall be as hateful and unprofitable
As that of truth is now.

               Where is the fame
Which the vain-glorious mighty of the earth
Seek to eternize? Oh! the faintest sound
From time's light footfall, the minutest wave
That swells the flood of ages, whelms in nothing
The unsubstantial bubble. Ay! to-day
Stern is the tyrant's mandate—red the gaze
That scatters multitudes. To-morrow comes,
That mandate is a thunder-peal that died
In ages past; that gaze, a transient flash
On which the midnight closed; and on that arm
The worm has made his meal.

                         PERCY BYSSHE SHELLEY.

NATURE'S NOBLEMAN.

Away with false fashion, so calm and so chill,
    Where pleasure itself cannot please;
Away with cold breeding, that faithlessly still
    Affects to be quite at its ease;
For the deepest in feeling is highest in rank,
    The freest is first in the band,
And nature's own nobleman, friendly and frank,
    Is a man with his heart in his hand!

Fearless in honesty, gentle, yet just,
    He warmly can love and can hate,
Nor will he bow down with his face in the dust,
    To fashion's intolerant state;
For best in good breeding, and highest in rank,
    Though lowly or poor in the land,
Is nature's own Nobleman, friendly and frank,
    The man with his heart in his hand!

His fashion is passion, sincere and intense,
    His impulses, simple and true;
Yet tempered by judgment, and taught by good sense,
    And cordial with me and with you;
For the finest in manners, as highest in rank,
    Is *you*, man! or *you*, man! who stand
Nature's own Nobleman, friendly and frank,
    A man with his heart in his hand!

                    MARTIN F. TUPPER.

THE WORLD FOR SALE.

The World For Sale!—Hang out the sign!
　Call every traveler here to me;
Who'll buy this brave estate of mine,
　And set me from earth's bondage free?
'Tis going!—yes, I mean to fling
　The bauble from my soul away;
I'll sell it, whatsoe'er it bring;
　The World at Auction here to-day!

It is a glorious thing to see—
　Ah, it has cheated me so sore!
It is not what it seems to be,
　For sale! It shall be mine no more.
Come, turn it o'er and view it well,
　I would not have you purchase dear;
'Tis *going! going!*—I must sell!
　Who bids?—Who'll buy the splendid Tear?

Here's Wealth in glittering heaps of gold—
　Who bids?—But let me tell you fair,
A baser lot was never sold;
　Who'll buy the heavy heaps of care?
And here, spread out in broad domain,
　A goodly landscape all may trace;
Hall, cottage, tree, field, hill, and plain,
　Who'll buy himself a burial-place?

Here's Love, the dreamy potent spell
　That beauty flings around the heart;
I know its power, alas! too well,
　'Tis *going!*—Love and I must part.
Must part?—What can I more with Love?
　All over the enchanter's reign;
Who'll buy the plumeless, dying dove,
　An hour of bliss—an age of pain?

And Friendship—rarest gem of earth—
    (Whoe'er hath found the jewel his?)
Frail, fickle, false, and little worth—
    Who bids for Friendship—as it is.
'Tis *going! going!*—Hear the call?
    Once, twice, and *thrice!*—'tis very low;
'Twas once my hope, my stay, my all,
    But now the broken staff must go!

Fame! hold the brilliant meteor high,
    How dazzling every gilded name;
Ye millions, now's the time to buy!
    How much for Fame?   How much for Fame?
Hear how it thunders!—Would you stand
    On high Olympus, far renown'd;
Now purchase, and a world command,
    And be with a world's curses crown'd!

Sweet star of Hope, with ray to shine
    In every sad foreboding breast,
Save this desponding one of mine,
    Who bids for man's last friend and best.
Ah, were not mine a bankrupt life,
    This treasure should my soul sustain;
But Hope and I are now at strife,
    Nor ever may unite again.

And Song!   For sale my tuneless lute,
    Sweet solace, mine no more to hold;
The chords that charm'd my soul are mute;
    I can not wake the notes of old!
Or e'en were mine a wizard shell,
    Could chain a world in rapture high;
Yet now a sad farewell!—farewell!
    Must on its last faint echoes die.

Ambition, fashion, show, and pride,
    I part from all forever now;

Grief, in an overwhelming tide,
  Has taught my haughty heart to bow.
Poor heart! distracted, ah, so long,
  And still its aching throb to bear;
How broken, that was once so strong,
  How heavy, once so free from care.

No more for me life's fitful dream,
  Bright vision, banishing away;
My bark requires a deeper stream,
  My sinking soul a surer stay.
By Death, stern sheriff! all bereft,
  I weep, yet humbly kiss the rod,
The best of all I still have left,
  My Faith, my Bible, and my God.

RALPH HOYT.

PROCRASTINATION.

If Fortune with a smiling face,
  Strew roses on our way;
When shall we stoop to pick them up?
  To-day, my friend, *to-day*.
But should she frown with face of care,
  And talk of coming sorrow;
When shall we grieve, if grieve we must?
  To-morrow, friend, *to-morrow*.

If those who've wronged us, own their fault,
  And kindly pity pray,
When shall we listen, and forgive?
  To-day, my friend, *to-day*.
But, if stern Justice urge rebuke,
  And warmth from Memory borrow,
When shall we chide, if chide we dare?
  To-morrow, friend, *to-morrow*.

If those to whom we owe a debt,
　Are harmed unless we pay,
When shall we struggle to be just?
　To-day, my friend, *to-day*.
But, if our debtor fail our hope,
　And plead his ruin thorough,
When shall we weigh his breach of faith?
　To-morrow, friend, *to-morrow*.

For virtuous acts, and harmless joys,
　The minutes will not stay;
We've always time to welcome them,
　To-day, my friend, *to-day*.
But care, resentment, angry words,
　And unavailing sorrow,
Come far too soon, if they appear
　To-morrow, friend, *to-morrow*.

　　　　　　　　　　CHARLES MACKAY.

NEVER DESPAIR.

This motto I give to the young and the old,
More precious by far than a treasure of gold;
'Twill prove to its owner a talisman rare,
More potent than magic—'tis *Never Despair!*

No, never despair, whatsoe'er be thy lot,
If Fortune's gay sunshine illumine it not;
Mid its gloom, and despite its dark burden of care,
If thou canst not be cheerful, yet, *Never Despair!*

Oh! what if the sailor a coward should be,
When the tempest comes down, in its wrath on the sea,
And the mad billows leap, like wild beasts from their lair,
To make him their prey, if he yield to *Despair?*

But see him amid the fierce strife of the waves,
When around his frail vessel the storm demon raves;
How he rouses his soul up to do and to dare!
And, while there is life left, will *Never Despair!*

Thou, too, art a sailor, and Time is the sea,
And life the frail vessel that upholdeth thee;
Fierce storms of misfortune will fall to thy share,
But, like the bold mariner, *Never Despair!*

Let not the wild tempest thy spirit affright,
Shrink not from the storm, though it come in its might;
Be watchful, be ready, for shipwreck prepare,
Keep an eye on the life-boat, and *Never Despair!*

WM. C. RICHARDS.

ADVICE TO A YOUNG MAN.

What would I have you do? I'll tell you, kinsman;
Learn to be wise, and practice how to thrive;
That would I have you do; and not to spend
Your coin on every bauble that you fancy,
Or every foolish brain that humors you.

I would not have you to invade each place,
Nor thrust yourself on all societies,
Till men's affections, or your own desert,
Should worthily invite you to your rank.
He that is so respectless in his courses,
Oft sells his reputation at cheap market.

Nor would I you should melt away yourself
In flashing bravery, lest, while you affect
To make a blaze of gentry to the world,
A little puff of scorn extinguish it,
And you be left like an unsavory snuff,
Whose property is only to offend.

I'd have you sober, and contain yourself;
Not that your sail be bigger than your boat;
But moderate your expenses now (at first),
As you may keep the same proportion still.
Nor stand so much on your gentility,
Which is an airy, and mere borrowed thing,
From dead men's dust and bones; and none of yours,
Except you make or hold it.

BEN JONSON.

ONWARD, ONWARD.

Onward! Orward is the language of creation! The stars whisper it in their courses; the seasons breathe it, as they succeed each other; the night wind whistles it; the water of the deep roars it out; the mountains lift up their heads, and tell it to the clouds; and Time, the hoary-headed potentate, proclaims it with an iron tongue! From clime to clime, from ocean to ocean, from century to century, and from planet to planet, all is onward.

From the smallest rivulet down to the unfathomable sea, every thing is onward. Cities hear its voice, and rise up in magnificence; nations hear it, and sink into the dust; monarchs learn it, and tremble on their thrones; continents feel it, and are convulsed with an earthquake.

Men, customs, fashions, tastes, opinions, and prejudices, are all onward. States, counties, towns, districts, cities, and villages are all onward, That word never ceases to influence the destinies of men. Science cannot arrest it, nor philosophy divert it from its purpose. It flows with the very blood in our veins, and every second of time chronicles its progress.

From one stage of civilization to another, from one towering landmark to another, from one attitude of glory to another, we still move upward and onward. Thus did our forefathers escape the barbarisms of past ages; thus do we conquer the errors of *our* time, and draw nearer to the invisible.

So must we move onward, with our armor bright, our weapons keen, and our hearts firm as the "everlasting hills." Every muscle must be braced, every nerve strung, every energy roused, and every thought watchful. *Onward* is the watchword! LINNÆUS BANKS.

THE CYNIC.

The Cynic is one who never sees a good quality in a man, and never fails to see a bad one. He is the human owl, vigilant in darkness, and blind to light, mousing for vermin, and never seeing noble game. The cynic puts all human actions into only two classes—*openly* bad, and *secretly* bad.

All virtue and generosity and disinterestedness are merely the *appearance* of good, but selfish at the bottom. He holds that no man does a good thing, except for profit. The effect of his conversation upon your feelings, is to chill and sear them; to send you away sour and morose. His criticisms and innuendoes fall indiscriminately upon every lovely thing, like frost upon flowers.

"Mr. A," says some one, "is a religious man." He will answer: "*Yes, on Sundays.*" "Mr. B has just joined the church:" "*Certainly; the elections are coming on.*" The minister of the gospel is called an example of diligence: "*It is his trade.*" Such a man is generous:—"*of other men's money.*" This man is obliging:—"*to lull suspicion and cheat you.*" That man is upright:—"*because he is green.*"

Thus, his eye strains out every good quality, and takes in only the bad. . To him religion is hypocrisy, honesty a preparation for fraud, virtue only want of opportunity, and undeniable purity, asceticism. The livelong day he will

sit with sneering lip, uttering sharp speeches in the quiet-
est manner, and in polished phrase, transfixing every character which is presented: *"His words are softer than oil,
yet are they drawn swords."*

All this, to the young, seems a wonderful knowledge of
human nature; they honor a man who appears to have
found out mankind. *They* begin to indulge themselves in
flippant sneers; and, with supercilious brow, and impudent tongue, wagging to an empty brain, call to naught
the wise, the long-tried, and the venerable.

I do believe that man is corrupt enough; but something
of good has survived his wreck; something of evil, religion has restrained, and something partially restored;
yet, I look upon the human heart as a mountain of fire. I
dread its crater. I tremble when I see its lava roll the
fiery stream.

Therefore, I am the more glad, if, upon the old crust of
past eruptions, I can find a single flower springing up. So
far from rejecting appearances of virtue in the corrupt
heart of a depraved race, I am eager to see their light, as
ever mariner was to see a star in a stormy night.

Moss will grow upon grave-stones; the ivy will cling to
the moldering pile; the mistletoe springs from the dying
branch; and, God be praised, something green, something
fair to the sight and grateful to the heart will yet twine
around, and grow out of the seams and cracks of the deso-
late temple of the human heart!

HENRY WARD BEECHER.

THE YANKEE BOY.

The Yankee boy, before he's sent to school,
Well knows the mysteries of that magic tool,
The pocket-knife. To that his wistful eye
Turns, while he hears his mother's lullaby;
His hoarded cents he gladly gives to get it,
Then leaves no *stone* unturned till he can whet it;
And, in the education of the lad,
No little part that implement hath had.

His pocket-knife to the young whittler brings
A growing knowledge of material things.
Projectiles, music, and the sculptor's art,
His chestnut whistle, and his shingle dart,
His elder pop-gun, with his hickory rod,
Its sharp explosion and rebounding wad;
His corn-stalk fiddle, and the deeper tone
That murmurs from his pumpkin-leaf trombone,
Conspire to teach the boy.

     To these succeed
His bow, his arrow of a feathered reed,
His wind-mill, raised the passing breeze to win,
His water-wheel, that turns upon a pin;
Or, if his father lives upon the shore,
You'll see his ship, beam ends upon the floor,
Full rigged, with raking masts and timbers staunch,
And waiting, near the washtub, for a launch.

Thus, by his genius and his jackknife driven,
Ere long he'll solve you any problem given;
Make any gimcrack, musical or mute,
A plow, a coach, an organ, or a flute;
Make you a locomotive, or a clock,
Cut a canal, or build a floating dock,
Or lead forth beauty from a marble block,

Make anything, in short, for sea or shore,
From a child's rattle to a seventy-four.
Make it, said I? Ay, when he undertakes it,
He'll make the thing, and the machine that makes it.

And, when the thing is made, whether it be
To move on earth, in air, or on the sea,
Whether on water, o'er the waves to glide,
Or upon land, to roll, revolve, or slide;
Whether to whirl or jar, to strike or ring,
Whether it be a piston or a spring,
Wheel, pulley, tube sonorous, wood or brass,
The thing designed shall surely come to pass;
For, when his hand's upon it, you may know
That there's *go* in it, and he'll *make* it go.

JOHN PIERPONT.

TRIBUTE TO GENIUS AND LABOR.

The camp has had its day of song;
  The sword, the bayonet, the plume,
Have crowded out of rhyme too long
  The plow, the anvil, and the loom.
Oh, not upon our tented fields
  Are Freedom's heroes bred alone,
The training of the workshop yields
  More heroes true than war has known.

Who drives the bolt, who shapes the steel,
  May, with the heart as valiant, smite,
As he who sees a foeman reel
In blood before his blow of might!
The skill that conquers space and time,
  That graces life, that lightens toil;
May spring from courage more sublime
  Than that which makes a realm its spoil.

Let Labor, then, look up and see
    His craft no path of honor lacks;
The soldier's rifle yet shall be
    Less honored than the woodman's ax.
Let Art his own appointment prize,
    Nor deem that gold or outward height
Can compensate the worth that lies
    In tastes that breed their own delight.

And may the time draw nearer still,
    When men this sacred truth shall heed,
That from the thought and from the will
    Must all that raises man proceed!
Though Pride should hold our calling low,
    For us shall duty make it good;
And we from truth to truth shall go,
    Till life and death are understood.

EPES SARGENT.

THE HOUR-GLASS.

Alas! how swift the moments fly!
    How flash the hours along;
Scarce here, yet gone already by,
    The burden of a song.
See childhood, youth, and manhood pass,
    And age with furrowed brow;
Time *was*—time *shall be*—drain the glass—
    But where in Time is Now?

Time is the measure but of change,
    No present hour is found;
The Past, the Future, fill the range
    Of Time's unceasing round.

Where then is *now?*   In realms above,
    With God's atoning Lamb,
In regions of eternal love,
    Where sits enthroned "I AM."

Then, Pilgrim, let thy joys and tears
    On Time no longer lean,
But, henceforth, all thy hopes and fears,
    From earth's affections wean.
To God let votive accents rise,
    With truth—with virtue live;
So all the bliss that Time denies,
    Eternity shall give.

                JOHN QUINCY ADAMS.

THE LOAN OF A LOVER.

A VAUDEVILLE, IN ONE ACT.

By J. R. PLANCHE,
Author of "THE CAPTAIN OF THE WATCH." ETC.

CHARACTERS.

Captain Amersfort.	Delve.
Peter Spyk.	Gertrude.
Swyzel.	Ernestine Rosendaal.

SCENERY.

SCENE.—Gardens of a villa on the canal near Utrecht. The tower of the cathedral is seen in the distance. In one corner of the gardens, overlooking the canal, is a summer-house, R., in the Dutch taste.

COSTUMES.

CAPTAIN AMERSFORT.—Officer's uniform.

PETER SPYK.—Nankeen jacket, flowered vest, full trunks, blue stockings, and Dutch hat.

SWYZEL.—Buff coat and trunks, figured vest, blue stockings and hat.

DELVE.—Brown jacket and trunks, striped stockings, and russet hat.

GERTRUDE.—Neat peasant's dress, with broad hat.—Second dress: Wedding dress of white muslin, trimmed with flowers.

ERNESTINE.—Silk spencer, white muslin dress, scarf, and Swiss straw hat.

PROPERTIES.

Note for Amersfort; note for Delve: clock to strike off
stage.

EXPLANATION OF THE STAGE DIRECTIONS.

The Actor is supposed to face the Audience.

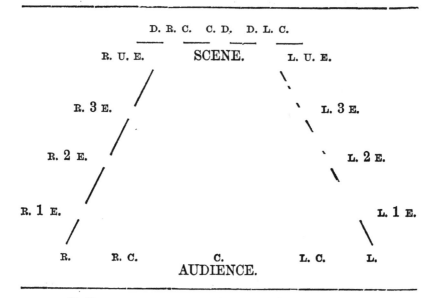

L.	Left.	c.	Center.
L. C.	Left Center.	R.	Right.
L. 1 E.	Left First Entrance.	R. 1 E.	Right First Entrance.
L. 2 E.	Left Second Entrance.	R. 2 E.	Right Second Entrance.
L. 3 E.	Left Third Entrance.	R. 3 E.	Right Third Entrance.
L U. E.	Left Upper Entrance.	R. U. E.	Right Upper Entrance.
	(wherever this Scene may be.)	D. R. C.	Door Right Center.
D. C. L.	Door Left Center.		

SYNOPSIS.

This charming little piece holds its own, both on the
stage and in the closet, in spite of the number of similar
pieces which have been since produced. In the garden of
a splendid villa, Swyzel and Delve, the former steward,

the other gardener to the rich and beautiful lady, ERNES-
TINE ROSENDAAL by name. The two are discussing the
projects and whims of their mistress, when PETER SPYK
joins them. The old steward expresses his surprise that
PETER does not get married, as he is a well-to-do young
farmer. SPYK answers that he has had thoughts of changing his condition, but somehow cannot fix upon any particular young woman, who is in all respects suitable.
PETER goes on to say, that he has consulted "little GER-
TRUDE" on the subject, and that she clearly explained to
him why there was not a solitary girl on his matrimonial
list, that would answer for his wife; one was too fat, another too lean; one too poor, another too rich; one too
frivolous, another too serious; and so on to the end of the
list. Both the STEWARD and SPYK, though they regard
"little GERTRUDE" as something of a simpleton, own that
she has very sensible ideas at times. Indeed, it was at her
suggestion that PETER now came to the villa to ask CAP-
TAIN AMERSFORT, (a visitor, and a suitor to the lady ERNES-
TINE,) to let him (SPYK) have a lease of his fine Appledoorn
farm. While they are talking, GERTRUDE comes running
in to tell the STEWARD that he was wanted to furnish wine
for the table. SWYZEL leaves them together, and GERTRUDE
tries all the innocent artifices of a natural-born coquette to
elicit a compliment or even a kind word from her cousin
PETER. But the stolid peasant is blind to her smiles, and
deaf to her words. Before leaving GERTRUDE, SPYK tells
her that if she can find him a suitable wife, he will make
her a present the day that he is married, and that she shall
dance at his wedding. A cheerful prospect for a girl who
is over head and ears in love with him. After he departs,
GERTRUDE gives vent to her feelings by singing a pretty
song, and retires to back of stage sobbing. ERNESTINE and
CAPTAIN AMERSFORT enter, and have a little dispute. He
is anxious to have the lady's promise to be his wife; but
she is not to be so easily won. ERNESTINE learns from the

weeping GERTRUDE, her maid and almost foster-sister, that
her grief is occasioned by the fact that she has no lover;
when the lady playfully suggests that as she has a super-
fluity of the by-no-means desirable article, she will give
the maid one of hers, and accordingly tenders the handsome CAPTAIN in that capacity. The village maid grate-
fully accepts the puzzled beau; but explains to the lady
that she only wants the *loan* of a lover, not the gift of one.
GERTRUDE contrives to awaken love in the heart of PETER
through his jealousy, when he sees that the officer is apparently in love with GERTRUDE. In this way the girl
brings PETER to make a declaration of his wish to marry
her. Meanwhile, the CAPTAIN, by skillfully playing the
lover, as ordered by his mistress, has awakened the jealous
feelings of the high-born lady, who quickly capitulates to
the gallant CAPTAIN, and general happiness is the result of
this "LOAN OF A LOVER."

THE PLAY.

SCENE.—*Gardens of a villa on the canal near Utrecht. The
tower of the cathedral is seen in the distance. In one corner of the garden, overlooking the canal, is a summer-
house,* R., *in the Dutch taste.*

Enter SWYZEL *and* DELVE, R.

SWYZEL. Do as you're bid, and no reflections. Don't
you know the mistress is the master?

DELVE. Well, but now really, Mynheer Swyzel—to put
out the orange trees before the white frosts are over—is
that common sense?

SWY. What have you to do with common sense? Nothing at all—or you would not pretend to have more than

your mistress.   It is Mamzelle Ernestine's pleasure to turn the orangery into a ball-room, and turned it must be.

DEL. But the trees will die.

SWY. Let 'em die, then—that's their business—yours is to clear the place out, according to order.   About it, without more words!   If she told me to fling all the Schiedam in the cellar into the canal, I should do so without hesitation.

DEL. You'd fling yourself after it, I'm sure.

SWY. Not when it was mixed with water, you rogue! or while the baron has money enough to buy more.   Come—to work! to work!   or you'll not get the room ready by midnight.

DEL. Oh, my poor orange trees—they'll die—every one of them.   (*Exit*, R.

SWY. Silly fellow, to trouble his head about what does not concern him.   If his employers take no care for their own interests, why should he fidget about them?   He hasn't the slightest notion of service!   Ah, here's Peter Spyk.

Enter PETER, L.

Well, Peter?

PETER. Good-morning, Master Steward.

SWY. So you've been to Amsterdam to buy cattle, I hear?

PETER. Ay, and fine beasts they are, too, Master Steward.   But, talking of beasts, how do you find yourself to-day?   You were rather poorly when I left.

SWY. Oh, I'm better, thank you, but I'm not so young as I was thirty years ago—I find that, Peter.   Ah, I envy you, you rogue!   Three-and-twenty — stout-timbered—light-hearted, and rich, I may say; for old Jan Spyk, your father, left you a pretty round sum, I take it?

PETER. Why, it might have been less, and yet worth having, Master Steward.

Swy. Well, and why don't you get a wife, now? All the girls in the neighborhood are pulling caps for you.

Peter. Why, I don't know; they do look at me, somehow, but I'm not smitten with anybody in particular. However, I don't wish to prevent them—they may fall in love with me, and then I can choose, you know.

Swy. Well, perhaps that's the best way.

Peter. Yes, I think so; as Gertrude said to me the other day, "You don't love anybody in particular, Peter, so you can look about you."

Swy. Gertrude—what, our Gertrude? The simpleton that has the run of the house and gardens by permission of the baron, because she's the orphan daughter of his old bailiff, and who is always so mighty busy, doing nothing at all, by way of earning the living allowed her! Is she your counselor?

Peter. Oh, she and I gossip now and then, when we meet. She's a sort of relation of mine; my brother-in-law's aunt stood grandmother to her.

Swy. Well, that is a sort of relation, certainly.

Peter. And then, you see, simpleton as she is, she has now and then an idea, and that's the only thing I want; I never have an idea. It's very odd, but I never have what you can really call an idea—of my own, that is—for I'm quick enough, if a person only just—and yesterday, now, I saw her but for two or three minutes, and I'll be hanged if she didn't give me a capital idea! and that's what has brought me here this morning. You've a Captain Amersfort staying here, haven't you?

Swy. Oh, yes; one of our young lady's score of lovers—and the best of 'em, too, to my mind; but she's too capricious to make up hers. He's a fine fellow—handsome, clever, gallant——

Peter. And landlord of the fine farm of Appledoorn—so Gertrude says.

Swy. Ah! and you want to be his tenant, no doubt?

PETER. Why, Gertrude thinks——

SWY. Well, she's right there; it's pretty property, but there are several farmers offering.

PETER. So she tells me; but she says that if you were to speak to the captain in my favor——

SWY. Well, she's right there, too. If I were to speak——

PETER. And will you, will you, Master Steward? I've a keg at home of the finest flavor, which I should be too happy——

SWY. Pshaw! pshaw! you know, if I do anything, it's never with a view to benefit myself, Peter; (*crosses*, R.) so send me the keg, if it will serve you, and we'll see what can be done about it.

GERTRUDE (*without*, L.) Mynheer Swyzel! Mynheer Swyzel!

SWY. Here comes Gertrude.

Enter GERTRUDE, *running*, L.

GER. Mynheer Swyzel! Mynheer Swyzel!

SWY. Well, don't bawl so, you young baggage. (*Crosses*, c.) What do you want?

GER. (*out of breath*). You're to go directly—I've been looking for you everywhere, to tell you—there's Peter Spyk.

SWY. To tell me that? why, I know that.

GER. No; to tell you—to tell you—how d'ye do, Peter? Are you very well? (*Crosses*, c.

PETER. Ay, ay!

SWY. Will you tell me what you mean to tell me?

GER. Law! I'd almost forgotten—I'd run so fast. How well Peter looks this morning, don't he?

SWY. Do let Peter alone! and tell me who wants me, and what for. Is it the wine for breakfast?

GER. Yes, that's it; you've got the keys of the cellar, and the baron wants some of the best Moselle, to give Captain Amersfort.

Swy. Good-morning, then, Peter. I'll take an opportunity of speaking to the captain, depend upon it. I must go now for the baron.

French Air.

GERTRUDE.

Well, but make more haste about it,
Master wants to treat his guest.

SWYZEL.

Oh, I'll please him—never doubt it!
Of his wines I know the best.
He shall own, that down his throttle,
Such has seldom found its way.

GERTRUDE (*aside*).
Then you'll get him up a bottle
Of what you drink every day. (*Exit* SWYZEL, L.

GER. (*aside*). An old rogue, I am sure he is; and he always snubs me and scolds me. So does everybody, indeed, except Peter. Peter never snubs me, at any rate; but that's because he hardly ever speaks to me. Now, only look at him this moment; there he stands, puffing away with his pipe, and turning up the whites of his eyes. Now, what can he be thinking about?—that is, if he is thinking; suppose it's about—(*aloud, and taking hold of his arm*) Peter!

PETER. Eh! Oh, you're here still, are you?

GER. (*aside*). How civil! (*Aloud*). Yes, I'm here still; and if I had kept still, you'd never have known it, seemingly. What are you thinking about so deeply?

PETER. Thinking about? Why, I was thinking about Mother Wynk's tavern, where I breakfasted this morning.

GER. What an interesting subject!

PETER. Rather. The old vrow worried my life out with, "Why don't you get married, Farmer Spyk?"—"Why do you live alone, in that old house, like an owl in an ivy-bush?"—"Why don't you take a wife—you've got money enough to keep one, and you are your own master; you've only to please yourself."

GER. Well, and haven't I told you so over and over again?

PETER. Well, so you have; and I do think, if I should get the Appledoorn farm, I'll sign a lease and a contract the same day.

GER. But, if you don't get the farm, what does it signify? You might marry all the same for that. You've enough without. You needn't wait; that is, if you like anybody well enough to marry them.

PETER. Ah, but then I don't know that I do. Now who is there, in your opinion, that would suit me?

GER. Oh, I don't know. I dare say, if I were to choose, I could name somebody.

PETER. Well, but let's see, now. To begin with the neighborhood: I know all the girls here, and I am sure I can't say. (*Suddenly.*) What d'ye think of Mary Moerdyke, to begin with?

GER. Very bad to begin with, and much better to have done with as soon as possible. She is the worst-tempered girl in all Utrecht, and as tall as the tower yonder; a great gawky, sulky thing, just like it.

PETER. Ah, well, I don't think she would suit me, certainly. But there's her cousin, Judith; she's very good-natured?

GER. Ah, Judith's a pretty girl, if you please, and very good-natured, as you say; perhaps a little too good-natured.

PETER. No, really—humph! I shouldn't like that. What do you say to Annie Stein?

GER. Everybody says she's a great coquette. See her on a Sunday, that's all! or at a dance at the fair! She's always changing her partner.

PETER. Oh, if she's always changing her partner—well, they can't say that of little Barbara?

GER. No, because she's lame, and can't dance at all!

PETER. That's very true; poor thing, she's lame, so she is. Well, I declare, then, Vrow Wynk herself?

GER. Old enough to be your grandmother.

PETER. And Rachel, her daughter?

GER. She's engaged to young Maurice.

PETER. The devil! Then I must go farther afield, for there's nobody else that I know of in this place.

GER. (aside). Oh, dear! oh, dear! how blind he is, to be sure!

PETER. Ah, stop! What a fool I am, never to have remembered——

GER. Well, who—what?

PETER. Why, that to-morrow will be market-day here, and that there'll be plenty of pretty girls from all the villages round about; so I can choose without the trouble of a journey.

Dutch Air.

PETER.

To-morrow will be market-day,
The streets all thronged with lasses gay,
And from a crowd so great, no doubt,
Sweethearts enough I may pick out.
    In verity, verity, etc.

GERTRUDE.

Be not too bold, for hearts fresh caught
Are ne'er, I'm told, to market brought;
The best, they say, are given away,
Nor left to sell on market day.
    In verity, verity, etc.

PETER. Well, at any rate, I'll take my chance of to-morrow. But yonder's mamzelle and some of the gentle-

folks, so I'll go and hear what the steward has done for
me. Good-by, Gertrude. I say, mind, if you can find
me a nice little, good-tempered wife, I'll make you a present the day I'm married, and you shall dance at the wedding.   (*Exit*, E.

GER. Now, isn't it provoking? He can think of everybody but me; and unless I were to say to him, plump,
"Peter, will you marry me?" and then, if he should say,
"No!" oh, I should die with shame and disappointment.
Oh, dear! oh, dear! how vexatious it is! And it's not
only Peter, but nobody seems to think me worth marrying
at all—nobody ever says a civil thing to me of any sort. I
never had a sweetheart in my life, and I do believe that's the
reason. If I only had one to begin with, I shouldn't wonder if they swarmed afterward!

SONG.

"*A Temple to Friendship.*"

I'm sure I'm not ugly! I'm only just twenty—
  I know I should make a most excellent wife;
The girls all around me have lovers in plenty,
  But I not a sweetheart can get for my life!

It isn't because I am not worth a penny,
  For lasses as poor I've known dozens to win;
That I should have none, and the others so many,
  I vow and declare it's a shame and a sin!

                          (*Retires up the stage, sobbing*, R.

Enter ERNESTINE *and* CAPTAIN AMERSFORT, L.

AMERSFORT. Why, you proposed the ride yourself,
Ernestine.

ERNESTINE. Perhaps I did, but I've changed my mind.
AMER. Will you walk, then?
ERN. It's too hot.
AMER. By the side of the canal—under the trees.

ERN. By the side of the canal? I wonder you don't propose I should tow the passage-boat!

AMER. I shouldn't wonder if you proposed something equally extravagant. For myself, I have done; I shall suggest nothing else. Please yourself, if possible, and you will please me.

ERN. Now he's out of humor.

AMER. No, not out of humor, but you are the most capricious creature!

ERN. Well, well, sir, if you are tired of your allegiance, renounce it at once. I have plenty of slaves at my footstool, who will serve me with oriental obedience.

AMER, (R.) If they really loved you, they would not encourage you in your follies.

ERN. (C.) My follies? How dare you talk to me of my follies, sir? Hold your tongue! Hold your tongue, directly! There's Gertrude, and I want to speak to her. Gertrude!
                                        (*Calling.*

GER. (L.) Yes, mamzelle.   (*Drying her eyes.*

ERN. What's the matter, Gertrude? you've been crying.

GER. (L.) Yes, mamzelle.

ERN. And what for? Has any one vexed you? some faithless swain, perhaps.

GER. Oh, dear, no, mamzelle. I wish it was, but that's not possible!   (*Bursts out afresh.*)

ERN. How d'ye mean—not possible, child?

GER. Because I haven't got a swain of any sort.

ERN. Bless the girl! What, no sweetheart, at your age?

GER. No, mamzelle.

ERN. Then perhaps that's what you're crying about?

GER. Yes, mamzelle.

ERN. Silly wench! you ought to rejoice at it rather; the men are nothing but plagues, Gertrude. Lovers, indeed! there's not one worth having.

GER. I—I wish I had one, though, just to try. I was just saying to myself, it was a shame that some young women should have a score, and others none at all.

AMER. The girl is right enough there. It is a shame that some young women should have a score, and hold out equal hopes to all.

ERN. The sooner you lessen the number of mine, the better, then. I could manage to spare even the gallant Captain Amersfort, and—a capital thought! as you seem so concerned at the unequal division, I'll transfer you to Gertrude.

GER. Law, mamzelle, you don't say so! Will you, really?

AMER. Ernestine! What folly!

ERN. I'm quite serious. As you have no admirer, Gertrude, and I have so many, I'll give you one of mine.

GER. Oh, but I don't want you to *give* me one, mamzelle. If you'll only lend me a beau—just to encourage the others.

ERN. Ha, ha, ha! delightful! That's better still!—you hear, sir; I am not to give you up altogether, though you deserve it; I shall only try your obedience! We command you, therefore, on pain of our sovereign displeasure, to pay all proper attentions to our handmaid, Gertrude; you are her beau till further notice.

AMER. Ernestine, are you mad?

ERN. Mad or not, you will obey me, or take the consequences. I won't be charged with folly and extravagance for nothing. (*Aside.*) Remember, I have promised my father to decide this day in favor of somebody. If you hesitate only, you are excluded from all chance. (*Aloud.*) Gertrude, I lend you a beau, on your personal security, mind.

GER. Oh, you needn't be afraid, mamzelle—I'll take the greatest care of him—and besides——

Dutch Air.

GERTRUDE.

Think not I the heart would **keep,**
  I'm content to borrow;
See if I don't have a heap
  To pay it from to-morrow.
Money, money makes, they say;
  The job is to get any;
And lovers grow—so money may——

ERNESTINE.

Oh, yes; one fool makes many.

ERN. (*to* AMERSFORT). One step, and you lose me forever.
                        (*Exit.*

AMER. (*to himself*). This passes everything. I am a fool, indeed, and love her like a fool, or I would never bear——

GER. Only think! I've got a beau at last—and such a beau! an officer—a fine young, handsome officer! What'll Peter say to that?

AMER. And while I thus humor her caprices, she returns to the house to flirt with that puppy, Amstell, or that booby, Blankenburg.

GER. But he takes no more notice of me than Peter himself.

AMER. I will not endure it. I will follow her, and——

GER, Stop! stop! you mustn't run away—you're only *lent* to me, you know; and if I should *lose* you, there'll be a pretty business!

AMER. (*Laughing in spite of himself.*) Upon my word, this is too ridiculous! So you really look upon me as a loan, do you?

GER. Yes, and I don't choose to be left alone. My stars! Peter could do that.

AMER. Peter! who's Peter? I thought you said you hadn't a sweetheart in the world.

GER. Nor have I.

AMER. Come, come, no fibs! You've betrayed yourself. This said Peter—isn't he a sweetheart?

GER. No, I don't think he is—at least, I don't know. What do you call a sweetheart—one whom you love, or one who loves you?

AMER. One who loves you, of course.

GER. Well, then, I'm right; he is not my sweetheart; but I am his, for I love him dearly.

AMER. What a candid little soul! And so you really love Peter dearly, though Peter doesn't love you? But are you sure he doesn't love you?

GER. I don't believe he ever thought about it.

AMER. Is it possible? Why, you are very pretty. (*Aside.*) Upon my soul, she is uncommonly pretty. I wonder I never noticed her before. (*Aloud.*) And so Peter has never thought about you?

GER. No——

SONG.

"Faut l' Oblier."

I've no money; so, you see,
Peter never thinks of me—
   I own it to my sorrow!
Oh, could I grow rich, and he
Be reduced to poverty,
What sweet revenge 'twould be for me
   To marry him to-morrow!
Peter's thought almost a fool,
You have profited by school—
   Wit from you folks borrow!
Peter's plain—you handsome, gay;
But if you were both to say—
"Will you have me, Gertrude, pray?"
   I'd marry *him* to-morrow!

AMER. There's love!—there's devotion! What charming

frankness!—what innocent enthusiasm! By Jove! if she wasn't so fond of another, I should be almost tempted—if it were only to punish Ernestine! I—I—(*aloud*) Confound that Peter! *Almost* a fool—he must be a downright idiot not to fall head over ears in love with such a sweet, dear, bewitching—(*catching her round the waist; he is about to kiss her as* PETER SPYK *enters with* SWYZEL.)

SWY. I beg your pardon, captain, (*both stop short*—PETER *staring at* GERTRUDE.)

GER. (*aside*).   Oh, lud, there *is* Peter.

AMER. What the devil do you want?

SWY. Only to introduce Peter Spyk—an honest young farmer—who desires to be your honor's tenant.

AMER. Peter Spyk! What, is this *the* Peter?

GER. Yes, that's Peter Spyk; and he wants to rent your farm of Appledoorn; and I am sure you can't do better than to let him have it, for he's as good a farmer, and as honest a young man——

AMER. If you interest yourself for him, my dear Gertrude, that is sufficient.   (*aside to* SWYZEL) Swyzel, come here—I am much interested about this girl!   I've taken a great fancy to her!

SWY. What, to our Gertrude?—to that poor, simple thing?   Well, I thought just now you seemed rather—eh? You're a terrible man, captain!   What will mamzelle say?

AMER. Oh, it's all in pure friendship, I assure you; but come this way, and tell me all you know about her. (*aloud to* PETER) I'll speak to you presently, young man. (AMERSFORT *and* SWYZEL *enter the summer-house,* R. S. E.)

GER. Peter, you'll have the farm!

PETER. No, shall I, though?   Well, I thought he said something like it; and because you asked him, too! I say, you and he seem great friends—he'd got his arm around your waist!

GER. Had he?—oh, yes, I believe he had.

PETER. Well, now, I've known you ever since you were

that high, and I'm sure I never put my arm round your waist!

GER. No, that you never did! But then, he's my sweetheart!

PETER. *Your* sweetheart?—yours? What, the Captain? Pshaw! you're joking!

GER. Joking!—indeed I'm not joking! What is there so strange in it, pray?

PETER. Why, in the first place he's mamzelle's sweetheart!

GER. Not now.

PETER. What, has he left her for you? Why, what can a rich officer like that see in a poor servant girl?

GER. Don't be a brute, Peter! If you can't see anything to like in me, it's no reason that others should not.

PETER. Me!—oh, that's a different affair; because you and I, you know, there's no such difference between us, and—oh, by the by, talking of that—I've been thinking of what you said to me, and I won't wait any longer—not even till to-morrow—I've fixed on Annie Stein. Her mother was here just now, on some business with old Swyzel, and something was dropped about my having the Appledoorn farm; and Swyzel says, she gave him a hint that her daughter Anne was very fond of me, and that decided me at once.

GER. It did?

PETER. Oh, yes; because, where a woman is really fond of one, you know—So directly I've settled with the Captain about the farm, I'll post off to Widow Stein's, and—well, what's the matter with you, Gertrude? Why, you are crying!

GER. Nothing—nothing! I wish you may be happy—that's all, Peter.

PETER. Thank ye—thank ye! It's very kind of you to cry for joy about me, I'm sure—and I won't forget my promise.

Re-enter AMERSFORT *and* SWYZEL *from the summer-house,*
R. S. E.

SWY. You can't be in earnest, Captain?

AMER. I tell you, there it is, in black and white! Put a
wafer in that (*giving a note*) and send it immediately to my
lawyer's, as directed.

SWY. Two thousand crowns to portion off a wench like
that. 'Gad, she won't want a husband long. [*Exit*, R.

AMER. (*to* PETER). Now for you, farmer. I find there
are writing materials in the summer-house, so we can——

GER. Stop! stop!—one word.

AMER. What is it?

GER. (*leading him apart from* PETER). You are my beau,
you know, and you're to do everything I bid you!

AMER. Of course.

GER. Well, then, I bid you refuse the farm to Peter
Spyk!

AMER. Refuse! Why, I thought you said——

GER. It doesn't signify what I said! I've changed my
mind! I suppose I may do that as well as your fine ladies!
You're to obey me! Mamzelle Ernestine said so, and I
don't choose you shall let Peter have the farm! (*speaking
the last five words loud enough for* PETER *to hear.*)

PETER (*aside*). "*Let Peter have the farm!*" Gad, she's
giving me a famous lift with the captain.

AMER. Well, if you don't choose, he sha'n't have it, certainly; and I'm not sorry, for I don't think he deserves it.
And now listen to me. I mean to help you to a good husband, and in return, you must assist me in a little plot. I
can't stay to tell you now; but meet me in half an hour's
time at the sun-dial yonder. May I depend upon you?

GER. That you may.

AMER. Enough! Now, (*crosses*, L.) Master Peter Spyk,
follow me. There's no occasion for writing; we can settle
this business in two words.

PETER (*aside*). The farm's mine! (*to* GERTRUDE) I owe
you a good turn for this.   [*Exit with* AMERSFORT, L.

GER. Indeed you do.   If Annie Stein marries him now,
I'm mistaken in the family altogether.

Re-enter SWYZEL, R.

SWY. I've sent Delve with the note; but I've made up
my mind.   I'm not a young man, certainly; and I had no
idea of changing my situation; but two thousand crowns
will suit me as well as any body in the world, and so here
goes—there's nothing like being first in the field. (*aloud*)
Gertrude! Gertrude!—come hither, Gertrude; I want to
say a word to you in private!

GER. To me, Master Steward? (*aside*) Oh, dear, now he's
going to scold me for something, I'm sure.   A cross old
patch!

SWY. Come here, I tell you!   Nearer—don't be afraid—
I'm going to propose something for your good, my dear!

GER. (*aside*). "My dear!"   Bless me, how kind he's
grown all of a sudden!

SWY. I've known you a long while, Gertrude—from your
cradle, in fact.   I knew your poor dear father and mother,
and I always had a great affection for you!

GER. You, Mynheer Swyzel? I'm sure you never showed
it, then.

SWY. May be not—may be not!   I was afraid of spoiling
you as a child; but now, you know, you are grown up,
and very nicely you have grown up—I see it more and
more every day—and, in short, Gertrude, I've been thinking that, as I am a bachelor, I couldn't do better than
marry a good, pretty girl like you, whose character and
temper I have watched the growth of from an infant.

GER. You—you, Mynheer Swyzel, marry me?

SWY. Why not—why not?—if you have no objection.
I'm only fifty-five, and a hale, hearty man for that age.   I
have saved some money in the service, and——

GER. But I haven't a doit in the world!

SWR. Nay—nay!—you are richer than you think for!

GER. Eh?

SWY. In charms—in youth and beauty!——

GER. (*aside*). So—so! here's a real, downright sweet-heart at last!—and old Swyzel, too, of all men in the world! I shall die of laughing!

SWY. (*aside*). She's silent!—she hesitates! The two thousand crowns are mine!

Dutch Air.

SWYZEL.

My ears with sweet contentment bless!

GERTRUDE (*aside*).

The moon must sure, be about full!

(*aloud*) I don't say *no*—I don't say *yes*.

SWYZEL.

Alack that's rather doubtful!

GERTRUDE.

What proofs have I you mean me fair?

Your sex is of deceit, throughout, full.

SWYZEL.

Upon my honor, I declare!

GERTRUDE.

Alack that's rather doubtful!

GER. (*aside*). Here's Peter coming back. If I could manage—(*aloud*) Besides, that isn't the way to swear you love a body—you should go down on your knees!

SWY. There!—there, then! (*kneels*) Charming Gertrude, on my knees I swear eternal love and constancy!

Enter PETER, L.

PETER. Halloo!—why, Mynheer Swyzel, what are you doing there?

SWY. (*scrambling up*). Confusion! (*aloud*) I—nothing—only kneeling to—(*aside to* GERTRUDE) Don't say nothing to that fool. Come to my room as soon as you've got rid of him.   [*Exit*, R.

GER. You here again, Peter?

PETER. Here again!—I believe I am, too; and just as I went away. Would you believe it?—Captain Amersfort won't let me have the farm after all.

GER. Dear me!—you don't say so?

PETER. He wouldn't hear a word; and, to make matters worse, old Widow Stein, who saw me talking to him, waited to hear the upshot; and, when I told her, she as good as gave me to understand that I wasn't match enough for her daughter, and that Annie herself liked Groot, the miller, much better than she did me! A coquette!—you said she was a coquette!—and you were quite right. I don't know how it is, but you're always right!—you've got more sense than all of 'em put together; and, for the matter of looks, why there's the captain's vows—and, talking of vows, what was old Swyzel about on his knees? I do believe he was vowing, too?

GER. Between you and me, he was vowing all sorts of love to me!—and he wants me to marry him!

PETER. Marry him!—marry old Swyzel!—and will you?

GER. I don't know!—what do you think? Would you like me to marry him, Peter?

PETER. Not at all! I don't know how it is, but I can't fancy your marrying anybody—that is, I never thought of *your* marrying anybody; and, now I think of it, I think——

GER. Well—what?

Enter DELVE, *with a note*, R.

DELVE. Oh, Gertrude, here you are; here's a note for you. It's very particular—they gave me a florin to run all the way!

GER. A note for me?—who is it from?

DELVE. The clerk at Van Nickem's, the lawyer. I took a letter there for the captain, and, as his master wasn't at home, the clerk opened it, and wrote this answer to the captain, and then scribbled that for you, and begged me to give you yours first—and so I have; and now I must find the captain.   [*Exit*, R.

GER. A note for me? Nobody ever wrote to me before; and, if they had, it would have been no use, for I can't read written hand. You can, Peter; so pray open it, and let's hear what it's all about.

PETER. (*opening and reading*). "*Mamzelle.*" Mamzelle, to you!

GER. Go on—go on.

PETER. "I have loved you above all earthly beings!"

GER. Bless us, and save us!

PETER. "I dared not disclose my passion; but, believe me, my affection was equal to my silence."

GER. Then it was great indeed!

PETER. "I have at length summoned courage to address you, and if the offer of my hand and fortune"—another proposal!—who is the fellow that writes this?

GER. Van Nickem's clerk, Delve told you.

PETER. Yes; here's his ugly name, sure enough, at the bottom of it—Simon Sneek!

GER. Ah! if I recollect, he's rather a good-looking young man.

PETER. Why, you don't mean to——

GER. Surely, he's better than old Swyzel!

PETER. Well, but what does it all mean? Everybody wants to marry you.

GER. I can't help that—can I? But I sha'n't be in a hurry; I shall do as you do—look about me; perhaps somebody may offer that I should like better. (*Clock strikes.*) Hark! that's two o'clock! (*Crosses*, L.) And I promised to meet the captain at the sun-dial yonder. Good-by, Peter; and mind, if you can find me a hus-

band that I should like better than any of these, I'll make
you a present the day I'm married, and you shall dance at
the wedding.   (*Runs out,* L.

PETER. (*stands staring after her, with the open note in his
hand*). Well, when she talks of Annie Stein always changing her partner—she's off to meet the captain now, and
yet she says to me, "If you can find me a husband I should
like better;" the idea of Gertrude having a husband!—a
little girl, that was only a baby the other day, as it seems
to me. I wonder if she'd like *me* better; because if she
would—I want a wife myself—and I don't know why I
didn't at first. But there goes that cursed captain, running like mad to meet her. Gad, I begin to feel that I
don't like it at all. Why can't he keep to his fine ladies,
and let the others alone? I don't go and make love to
Mamzélle Érnestine, do I? What business has he to talk
a pack of stuff to Gertrude, and turn the poor girl's head?
He'd better mind what he's about, though; I can tell him
that! If he makes her unhappy, I wouldn't be in his
shoes for something, for I should break every bone in my
own skin!

Enter DELVE, R.

DEL. What's the matter, Master Peter? you don't look
pleased.

PETER. Well, I have been pleased better.

DEL. Anything in that note?

PETER. This note? no. This is the note you brought
from Van Nickem's. There's that young rogue, Sneek,
wants to marry Gertrude.

DEL. To marry Gertrude? well, now, do you know, I
think he might do worse.

PETER. Might do worse? I believe he might, too.

DEL. Gertrude's by no means ill-looking.

PETER. Ill-looking? she's very pretty!

DEL. Well, yes, I think she is; and very good-tempered.

PETER. The best-humored soul in the world.

DEL. Do you know, Master Peter, if I thought there was any chance of our living comfortably together, I shouldn't mind making up to Gertrude myself?

PETER. You?—you be hanged!

DEL. Hanged? what for, I should like to know? I question, now, if I couldn't afford to marry as well as young Sneek; he doesn't get much out of Van Nickem's pocket, I'll swear.

PETER. Well, you needn't trouble your head about it, because you sha'n't have her.

DEL. Why, Farmer Spyk, what have you to do with it? Suppose I choose, and she chooses, you're neither her father nor her mother. If you put my blood up, I'll go and ask her at once.

PETER. And if you do, you'll put *my* blood up, and then I shall knock you down.

DEL. Knock me down? Donner and blitzen!

PETER. Don't provoke me! I'm getting desperate—I mean to marry Gertrude myself, if she'll have me, and I'll fight anybody for her, with fists, knives, pistols—anything!

Enter ERNESTINE, R.

ERN. Heyday! heyday! what is all this noise about, and threat of fighting?

DEL. It's Farmer Spyk here, and please you, mamzelle, he threatens to knock me down, if I go a-courting to Gertrude; and all in an honest way, too. I'll be hanged if I don't go and ask her right away!   (*Exit*, L.

ERN. To Gertrude? why, how long have you taken this fancy into your head?

PETER. Why, not five minutes, mamzelle, and he has the impudence to set himself up against me, who have been in love with her—more than half an hour.

ERN. And where is the fair object of your contention? What does she say to these sudden passions?

PETER. I'm waiting to know what she'll say to mine—

but she's a plaguey long time with the captain. He's the only rival I'm afraid of; she seems dused fond of him, and he raves about her.

ERN. (*alarmed*). He does? (*Recovering herself.*) But, of course—I desired him.

PETER. You desired him, mamzelle?

ERN. Yes, I commanded him to make love to her.

PETER. Well, he won't be broke for disobedience, then —that's all I can say—for he does make love to her most furiously. I caught them myself with his arm around her waist, this morning, and I dare say it's round it now, if the truth was known; but I can't see, for that beastly holly-bush.

ERN. Why, where are they, then?

PETER. She was to meet him at the sun-dial, and I saw him slinking through the trees yonder; and just now I'm almost certain I caught a glimpse of them at the end of that walk.

ERN. (*aside*). I don't like this account; I'm afraid I've acted very silly. I repented of the freak almost as soon as I left them, but my pride would not suffer me to return. The girl's pretty—very pretty; and if Amersfort, enraged at my indifference, should, out of mere spite—such things have happened—oh, dear, I do not like it at all.

PETER. There she goes! there she goes!

ERN. With the captain?

PETER. No, by herself; and there's Delve after her as hard as he can scamper! I'll follow—I'll—no, I can't—I can't move—I—I feel very ill—my head spins round like a top. Here comes the captain!

ERN. Amersfort? I am ready to sink!

PETER. Don't—don't—mamzelle, for I've no strength to catch you!

Enter AMERSFORT, L.

AMER. (*aside*). She is here—now for the trial. Mademoiselle Ernestine, I came to seek you.

ERN. Indeed, sir; and for what purpose? I thought I had desired you to pay your attentions in another quarter for the present.

AMER. It is in perfect accordance with that desire that I have sought this interview. I am anxious to express my gratitude for the blessing which you have so unexpectedly bestowed on me.

ERN. What do you mean, sir?

AMER. I mean, Mademoiselle Rosendaal, that the heart you treated with so much indifference has been accepted by one of the most lovely and amiable of your sex; and that, in the affection of Gertrude it has found a balm for all the wounds you had so wantonly inflicted on it.

PETER. There, there! I told you so!

ERN. Upon my word, sir! and you have the assurance to make this confession to me?

AMER. Why not, mademoiselle? We are not masters of our own affections, and therefore I will not reproach you. But can you be surprised that I should weary of loving one who did not love me? or that, stung to the quick by your contempt, I should be more sensible to the kindness and sympathy of another? Gertrude is lovely!

PETER. She is! she is!

AMER. The sweetest tempered — the most frank and affectionate of beings!

PETER. Too true! too true!

AMER. The possession of her heart is a blessing monarchs might envy me.

PETER. I shall go mad!

AMER. And monarchs have matched with maidens as lowly born, and far less deserving.

ERN. Enough—enough, sir!

PETER. No, it's not enough! he can't say too much about her. She hasn't her equal upon earth.

AMER. You are right, farmer; and I thank you for the honest warmth with which you justify my choice.

PETER. Your choice? Don't touch me!

AMER. My sweet bride—my affianced wife—Madame Amersfort will thank you in person.

PETER. His wife! Madame Amersfort! Cruel, faithless Gertrude!

AMER. Faithless? why, did you ever propose to her?

PETER. No, but I meant to do so. Oh, dear!

ERN. Your wife—your wife? And you really intend to marry this orphan girl?

AMER. I have desired my lawyer to prepare her marriage contract, which shall be signed this evening.

PETER. Oh!

ERN. Not in this house, sir! I will not be insulted to that extent. I go this moment to inform my father!

AMER. The Baron Van Rosendaal is already informed, and approves of my intentions.

ERN. Approves? We shall see, sir, we shall see!

AIR.—(*From "The Challenge."*)

ERNESTINE.

Such perfidy never was known,
I joy in its unmasking!

PETER.

Oh, Gertrude, you've a heart of stone,
To break a heart so true!

AMERSFORT.

Why, had she promised you?

PETER.

No, there's her falsehood shown!
So bent was she on jilting me,
She could not wait for asking.

AMERSFORT.

Well, there with you I must agree,

Such falsehood ne'er was known;
I'm sure with me you must agree,
Such falsehood ne'er was known.

ERNESTINE.

'Tis well, 'tis well, sir; we shall see —
Such falsehood ne'er was known.   [*Exit*, R.

AMER. (*aside*). Yes, yes, my fair tyrant, your father is in the plot; I think we have you now. (*Aloud*). Well, my good friend, I must say I pity you extremely; you have lost a model of a wife.

PETER. Don't! don't!

AMER. But where is she? where is my adored Gertrude?

Enter GERTRUDE, L. S. E., *dressed as a bride.* AMERSFORT *makes signs to her not to speak, and points to* PETER, *who stands in an attitude of comic despair. with his back toward them.*

I must hasten to find her.   I cannot bear to be an instant from her sight.   Oh, Peter, Peter! what a treasure has escaped you!   (*Exit*, R., *exchanging signs with* GERTRUDE.

PETER (*soliloquizing*). Escaped me! as if it were a mad dog, and it was an escape for Gertrude!   An escape! and I have let her escape!   Well, well, she won't be Madame Swyzel, or Madame Sneek; and that rascal Delve hasn't got her, that's one comfort.   Comfort?   I talk of comfort!   I shall never know comfort again!   Oh, Gertrude!   Gertrude!

GER. (*advancing*, R.). Did you call me, Peter?

PETER. Ha! what do I see?   There's a dress—a wedding-dress!   It is! it is!

GER. It is, it is a beautiful dress, as you say, and I don't wonder you start to see me in such a dress; but as the bride of the captain, you know——

PETER. (L.) It is true, then, you are going—going to marry Captain Amersfort?

GER. Ah, he has told you, then? Well, I was in hopes of giving you an agreeable surprise.

PETER. An agreeable surprise?

GER. Why, are you not delighted, Peter, at my good fortune?

PETER. Delighted?

GER. Only think! a poor orphan girl like me, whom nobody loved, and nobody cared about——

PETER. It isn't true! I cared about you—I doted on you!

GER. You, Peter, you? Mercy on me! And why didn't you tell me so, then?

PETER. Because I didn't know it myself, then; but I do now, Gertrude, I do now.

GER. Now? now that it is too late?

PETER. But is it—is it too late? You are not married yet.

GER. No, but I have promised. The contract is ordered, and this beautiful dress was bought by the captain on purpose. You would not have me behave so shamefully to one who loves me dearly?

PETER. But I—I love you dearly.

GER. Ah, if you had but said so an hour ago! But you thought of everybody but me.

PETER. I know it—I know it. But then nobody thought of you, and now everybody does, and it proves to me that you—you are the only girl in the world that I ought to marry; and if you won't have me, I—I know what I'll do.

GER. Dear, me, Peter, what?

PETER. I'll fling myself into the canal.

GER. Nonsense!

PETER. You see if I don't then. I'm not desperate till I take anything in my head; but then nothing can turn me.

AIR.—("*Take care of the corner*".)

PETER.

I rush to my fate,
And my funeral straight-
Way shall follow my latest transgression,
And in the church-yard
It shall go very hard
But it meets with your bridal procession;
When my coffin appears,
You will melt into tears,
And your friends in your grief will be sharers.

GERTRUDE.

Oh, yes, not only I,
But my husband will cry—
"Stand out of the way," to the bearers!

PETER. Laughed at! I'll jump over the wall, here, into the canal, before your face.

GER. Indeed you sha'n't. Peter, don't be a fool, (*trying to hold him*). Oh dear, he will! Murder! help!

Enter ERNESTINE, R.

ERN. What's the matter now?

GER. Oh, mamzelle, help me to hold Peter. He wants to drown himself.

ERN. He is sillier than ever I supposed him, if he would drown himself for so worthless a person. I wonder you are not ashamed to look me in the face.

GER. I'm very sorry, mamzelle. I know you only lent me a lover; but how can I give you him back, if he won't go?

ERN. Cease your impertinence. Your simplicity is all affected.

GER. I'm sure, mamzelle, if the captain will only consent, I'll give him up with pleasure.

PETER. You will?

ERN. You will? Hark ye, Gertrude! Don't think that I care the least about Captain Ameisfort—his behavior has entirely destroyed any little affection I might have had for him; but only to vex him in my turn, if you will promise not to marry him——

PETER. Do, do.

ERN. I will settle a handsome income on you.

PETER. There! there!

ERN. Tell him that you do not love him.

PETER. Yes, yes.

ERN. That you love another—anybody.

PETER. Yes, me! I'm ready to be loved.

GER. (*aside*). I see him!—now's the time. (*aloud*) Well, mamzelle, I believe it would be only the truth—I have a great respect for Captain Amersfort, but I certainly do not love him—and perhaps I do love somebody else, (*looking at* PETER.)

PETER. Oh, Gertrude!

Enter AMERSFORT, *unseen by them*, L. U. E.

GER. But how can I consent to make him wretched? If there was any chance of your making it up—if I thought you still loved the captain, and you would make him happy in the avowal——

ERN. Would that decide you?

PETER (*to* ERNESTINE). Oh, do, then—do!

ERN. What would you have me say?

GER. That you forgive him, and are willing to marry him, if I give him up.

ERN. Well, then, I am willing.

AMER. (*taking her hand*). And so am I!

GER. And so am I.

PETER. Hurrah!

ERN. Captain Amersfort here? This was a plot, then?

AMER. Own that it was to secure your happiness, Ernestine, and you make mine forever.

ERN. Well, I believe I deserved this lesson.

PETER. And I'm sure I did.

GER. You've made up your mind, then, that I shall marry you now?

PETER. To be sure I have.

GER. Well, as you say, when you once *do* take a thing in your head, nothing can turn you, I suppose its useless to say "No." There is my hand, dear Peter.

AMER. And I suppose I may let him have the farm now.

GER. If you please, captain.

AMER. And give him the two thousand crowns that I desired Van Nickem to settle on you as a wedding portion?

PETER. Ah! then that's why young Sneek--but no matter.

FINALE.—(*Trio, from* "*The Challenge.*")

PETER, GERTRUDE, AND ERNESTINE.

She }
He } is mine.   She }
He } is mine. Let the stars work their will,
If our patrons approve, nothing now can go ill;
But the lover we lend must with them make his way,
Or our dealings will end with the devil to pay

ERNESTINE.

Should they not then befriend us?

GERTRUDE.

I will hope for the best,
If one kind friend will lend us
His hands to move the rest.
Will you ask?

PETER.

Say do you

GERTRUDE (*to the audience*).

Do you like it?

PETER.

Say do you.

ALL.

Oh, happy hour! Oh, joyous night!
Our patrons share in our delight.

She ⎫
He ⎬ is mine.   Let the stars work their will.
    ⎭

Since our friends have approved, nothing now can go ill.
The lover we lent has with them made his way,
And their smiles of content all our toils overpay.

Disposition of the characters at the fall of the Curtain.

AMERSFORT.   ERNESTINE.   GERTRUDE.   PETER

CURTAIN.

STREET & SMITH'S SELECT SERIES No. 23.

Price, 25 Cents.

Some Opinions of the Press.

"As the probabilities are remote of the play 'The Old Homestead' being seen anywhere but in large cities it is only fair that the story of the piece should be printed. Like most stories written from plays it contains a great deal which is not said or done on the boards, yet it is no more verbose than such a story should be, and it gives some good pictures of the scenes and people who for a year or more have been delighting thousands nightly. Uncle Josh, Aunt Tildy, Old Cy Prime, Reuben, the mythical Bill Jones, the sheriff and all the other characters are here, beside some new ones. It is to be hoped that the book will make a large sale, not only on its merits, but that other play owners may feel encouraged to let their works be read by the many thousands who cannot hope to see them on the stage."—*N. Y. Herald*, June 2d.

"Denman Thompson's 'The Old Homestead' is a story of clouds and sunshine alternating over a venerated home; of a grand old man, honest and blunt, who loves his honor as he loves his life, yet suffers the agony of the condemned in learning of the deplorable conduct of a wayward son; a story of country life, love and jealousy, without an impure thought, and with the healthy flavor of the fields in every chapter. It is founded on Denman Thompson's drama of 'The Old Homestead.'"—*N. Y. Press*, May 26th.

"Messrs. Street & Smith, publishers of the *New York Weekly*, have brought out in book-form the story of 'The Old Homestead,' the play which, as produced by Mr. Denman Thompson, has met with such wondrous success. It will probably have a great sale, thus justifying the foresight of the publishers in giving the drama this permanent fiction form."—*N. Y. Morning Journal*, June 2d.

"The popularity of Denman Thompson's play of 'The Old Homestead' has encouraged Street & Smith, evidently with his permission, to publish a good-sized novel with the same title, set in the same scenes and including the same characters and more too. The book is a fair match for the play in the simple good taste and real ability with which it is written. The publishers are Street & Smith, and they have gotten the volume up in cheap popular form."—*N. Y. Graphic*, May 29.

"Denman Thompson's play, 'The Old Homestead,' is familiar, at least by reputation, to every play-goer in the country. Its truth to nature and its simple pathos have been admirably preserved in this story, which is founded upon it and follows its incidents closely. The requirements of the stage make the action a little hurried at times, but the scenes described are brought before the mind's eye with remarkable vividness, and the portrayal of life in the little New England town is almost perfect. Those who have never seen the play can get an excellent idea of what it is like from the book. Both are free from sentimentality and sensation, and are remarkably healthy in tone."—*Albany Express.*

"Denman Thompson's 'Old Homestead' has been put into story-form and is issued by Street & Smith. The story will somewhat explain to those who have not seen it the great popularity of the play."—*Brooklyn Times*, June 8th.

"The fame of Denman Thompson's play, 'Old Homestead,' is world-wide. Tens of thousands have enjoyed it, and frequently recall the pure, lively pleasure they took in its representation. This is the story told in narrative form as well as it was told on the stage, and will be a treat to all, whether they have seen the play or not."—*National Tribune*, Washington, D. C.

"Here we have the shaded lanes, the dusty roads, the hilly pastures, the peaked roofs, the school-house, and the familiar faces of dear old Swanzey, and the story which, dramatized, has packed the largest theater in New York, and has been a success everywhere because of its true and sympathetic touches of nature. All the incidents which have held audiences spell-bound are here recorded—the accusation of robbery directed against the innocent boy, his shame, and leaving home; the dear old Aunt Tilda, who has been courted for thirty years by the mendacious Cy Prime, who has never had the courage to propose; the fall of the country boy into the temptations of city life, and his recovery by the good old man who braves the metropolis to find him. The story embodies all that the play tells, and all that it suggests as well."—*Kansas City Journal,* May 27th.

THE COUNTY FAIR.

By NEIL BURGESS.

Written from the celebrated play now running its second continuous season in New York, and booked to run a third season in the same theater.

The scenes are among the New Hampshire hills, and picture the bright side of country life. The story is full of amusing events and happy incidents, something after the style of our "Old Homestead," which is having such an enormous sale.

"THE COUNTY FAIR" will be one of the great hits of the season, and should you fail to secure a copy you will miss a literary treat. It is a spirited romance of town and country, and a faithful reproduction of the drama, with the same unique characters, the same graphic scenes, but with the narrative more artistically rounded, and completed than was possible in the brief limits of a dramatic representation. This touching story effectively demonstrates that it is possible to produce a novel which is at once wholesome and interesting in every part, without the introduction of an impure thought or suggestion. Read the following

OPINIONS OF THE PRESS:

Mr. Neil Burgess has rewritten his play, "The County Fair," in story form. It rounds out a narrative which is comparatively but sketched in the play. It only needs the first sentence to set going the memory and imagination of those who have seen the latter and whet the appetite for the rest of this lively conception of a live dramatist.—*Brooklyn Daily Eagle.*

As "The County Fair" threatens to remain in New York for a long time the general public out of town may be glad to learn that the playwright has put the piece into print in the form of a story. A tale based upon a play may sometimes lack certain literary qualities, but it never is the sort of thing over which any one can fall asleep. Fortunately, "The County Fair" on the stage and in print is by the same author, so there can be no reason for fearing that the book misses any of the points of the drama which has been so successful.—*N. Y. Herald.*

The idea of turning successful plays into novels seems to be getting popular. The latest book of this description is a story reproducing the action and incidents of Neil Burgess' play, "The County Fair." The tale, which is a romance based on scenes of home life and domestic joys and sorrows, follows closely the lines of the drama in story and plot.—*Chicago Daily News.*

Mr. Burgess' amusing play, "The County Fair," has been received with such favor that he has worked it over and expanded it into a novel of more than 200 pages. It will be enjoyed even by those who have never heard the play and still more by those who have.—*Cincinnati Times-Star.*

This touching story effectively demonstrates that it is possible to produce a novel which is at once wholesome and interesting in every part, without the introduction of an impure thought or suggestion.—*Albany Press.*

Street & Smith have issued "The County Fair." This is a faithful reproduction of the drama of that name and is an affecting and vivid story of domestic life, joy and sorrow, and rural scenes.—*San Francisco Call.*

This romance is written from the play of this name and is full of touching incidents.—*Evansville Journal.*

It is founded on the popular play of the same name, in which Neil Burgess, who is also the author of the story, has achieved the dramatic success of the season.—*Fall River Herald.*

The County Fair is No. 33 of "The Select Series," for sale by all Newsdealers, or will be sent, on receipt of price, **25 cents,** to any address, postpaid, by **STREET & SMITH,** Publishers, 25-31 Rose st., New York.

ANOTHER MAN'S WIFE.

An Entrancing Emotional Story,

By BERTHA M. CLAY.

No. I of the Primrose Edition of Copyright Novels.

Cloth. Price, $1.

SOME OPINIONS OF THE PRESS.

Messrs. Street & Smith, New York, begin a new series of novels—"The Primrose Library"—with "Another Man's Wife," by Bertha M. Clay. The story has enough plot to keep one from falling asleep over it, and it also indicates the stumbling-blocks and pitfalls which abound everywhere for young husbands and wives who think so much about having "a good time" that they have no time left in which to think about reputation and character.—*N. Y. Herald*, Sept. 10.

Street & Smith publish the American copyright novel, "Another Man's Wife," by Bertha M. Clay. It deals with certain corrupting influences of fashionable society, and impressively warns of the dangers that spring from them. Its plot is strong and dramatic, and is elaborated with all of the qualities of style that have made the author so popular. It is the first issue of the new Primrose Series.—*Boston Globe*, Sept. 16.

"Another Man's Wife," by Bertha M. Clay, Street & Smith's Primrose Series, is a laudable effort toward the repression of the growing evil of matrimonial disloyalty. The book is handsomely bound, with a holiday look about it.—*Brooklyn Eagle*, Sept. 15.

Street & Smith of New York publish in cloth cover "Another Man's Wife," by Bertha M. Clay. The story is effective. It impressively depicts the results certain to attend the sins of deception. It teaches a lesson that will not be lost upon those thoughtless men and women who, only intent upon pleasure, little dream of the pitfall before them, and to which they are blind until exposure wrecks happiness.—*Troy (N. Y.) Press.*

Street & Smith, New York, have brought out in book-form "Another Man's Wife." This is one of Bertha M. Clay's most effective stories.—*Cincinnati Enquirer.*

"Another Man's Wife." This is one of Bertha M. Clay's most effective stories. It forcibly and impressively portrays the evils certain to attend matrimonial deceit, clandestine interviews, and all the tricks and devices which imperil a wife's honor. It has a novel and entrancingly interesting plot, and abounds in vivid and dramatic incidents. It is the first issue of Street & Smith's Primrose Edition of Copyright Novels; and will not appear elsewhere.—*Franklin Freeman.*

A LIST OF

AMERICAN LADIES

WHO HAVE

Married Foreigners of Rank.

ILLUSTRATED WITH ARMORIAL BEARINGS.

STREET & SMITH'S

HAND-BOOK LIBRARY.—No. 3.

Price 50 Cents.

SOME OPINIONS OF THE PRESS:

The title page of this volume is not sufficiently long, for besides all it promises it neglects to announce that there is also a list of available noblemen who have have not yet entered the state of matrimony, and to whom, presumably, American beauty backed by American gold may successfully appeal.—*N. Y. Herald, March* 16.

The book is remarkably complete and is valuable as a reference, in addition to being decidedly interesting.—*N. Y. World, March* 18.

The book gives all the attainable facts and figures concerning rich American girls who have married foreigners of more or less distinction.—*N. Y. Sun, March* 14.

In fact "Titled Americans" is a book that should be in the hands of each unmarried female in this country, and from it she should learn the glorious destiny that she may achieve.—*Munsey's Weekly.*

It furnishes a great deal of information, which will be valuable for reference, concerning American ladies who have married titled foreigners.—*Boston Saturday Evening Gazette.*

Of course American "gentlemen" cannot "come in" when such a book is produced. They will have to wait until some century when women rule Europe and carry all the purchasable titles in their own right.—*Brooklyn Daily Eagle.*

Embraced in this carefully compiled book, which is vastly entertaining in its way, are personal sketches of all the bachelor peers of Britain. We take it that the moral of the work for our American maidens is, "Go thou and do likewise," and that its mission is to show them where and how.—*Boston Times.*

Here is a volume for which young American women will be truly grateful. It contains the names of two hundred and five American girls who have married foreigners. This is of course very exciting reading, and will probably keep many girls awake at night, planning to go and do likewise.—*Pittsburgh Bulletin, March* 15.

"Titled Americans" is a valuable and unique work of considerable labor and expense, and something every person in society will be interested in.—*N. Y. Evening Telegram, March* 13.

Street & Smith have issued a rather unique book, but one that, in these days when titled foreigners are gobbling up and carrying off so many American belles and rich girls, will not be without use for reference —*Detroit Tribune.*

The only book of the kind ever published This is an interesting and unique work of considerable labor and expense, and something many society people will be interested in, as it gives a complete record to date of all American ladies who have married titled foreigners, illustrated with their armorial bearings. Young ladies traveling abroad should not fail to secure a copy as it will be of great assistance in regulating their heart strings.—*Elmira Telegram.*

If anything were needed to crystallize the craze of some American women for titled husbands it has been provided in this veritable hand-book for marriageable maidens and ambitious widows. It will doubtless be hidden away in some secret corner of the boudoir, or carried off in the traveling trunk across the ocean, to be consulted, cherished and studied; while the names of more than two hundred American women who have successfully hunted down the titled game will arouse the envy and hasten the palpitation of many a husband-hunting aspirant to wedded privileges —*N. Y. Saturday Review, March* 8.

THE SELECT SERIES

OF

POPULAR AMERICAN COPYRIGHT STORIES.

No. 47—SADIA THE ROSEBUD, by Julia Edwards............
No. 46—A MOMENT OF MADNESS, by Charles J. Bellamy............
No. 45—WEAKER THAN A WOMAN, by Charlotte M. Brame............
No. 44—A TRUE ARISTOCRAT, by Mrs. Georgie Sheldon............
No. 43—TRIXY, by Mrs. Georgie Sheldon............
No. 42—A DEBT OF VENGEANCE, by Mrs. E. Burke Collins............
No. 41—BEAUTIFUL RIENZI, by Annie Ashmore............
No. 40—AT A GIRL'S MERCY, by Jean Kate Ludlum............
No. 39—MARJORIE DEANE, by Bertha M. Clay............
No. 38—BEAUTIFUL BUT POOR, by Julia Edwards............
No. 37—IN LOVE'S CRUCIBLE, by Bertha M. Clay............
No. 36—THE GIPSY'S DAUGHTER, by Bertha M. Clay............
No. 35—CECILE'S MARRIAGE, by Lucy Randall Comfort............
No. 34—THE LITTLE WIDOW, by Julia Edwards............
No. 33—THE COUNTY FAIR, by Neil Burgess............
No. 32—LADY RYHOPE'S LOVER, by Emma Garrison Jones............
No. 31—MARRIED FOR GOLD, by Mrs. E. Burke Collins............
No. 30—PRETTIEST OF ALL, by Julia Edwards............
No. 29—THE HEIRESS OF EGREMONT, by Mrs. Harriet Lewis............
No. 28—A HEART'S IDOL, by Bertha M. Clay............
No. 27—WINIFRED, by Mary Kyle Dallas............
No. 26—FONTELROY, by Francis A. Durivage............
No. 25—THE KING'S TALISMAN, by Sylvanus Cobb, Jr............
No. 24—THAT DOWDY, by Mrs. Georgie Sheldon............
No. 23—DENMAN THOMPSON'S OLD HOMESTEAD............
No. 22—A HEART'S BITTERNESS, by Bertha M. Clay............
No. 21—THE LOST BRIDE, by Clara Augusta............
No. 20—INGOMAR, by Nathan D. Urner............
No. 19—A LATE REPENTANCE, by Mrs. Mary A. Denison............
No. 18—ROSAMOND, by Mrs. Alex. McVeigh Miller............
No. 17—THE HOUSE OF SECRETS, by Mrs. Harriet Lewis............
No. 16—SIBYL'S INFLUENCE, by Mrs. Georgie Sheldon............
No. 15—THE VIRGINIA HEIRESS, by May Agnes Fleming............
No. 14—FLORENCE FALKLAND, by Burke Brentford............
No. 13—THE BRIDE ELECT, by Annie Ashmore............
No. 12—THE PHANTOM WIFE, by Mrs. M. V. Victor............
No. 11—BADLY MATCHED, by Mrs. Helen Corwin Pierce............
No. 10—OCTAVIA'S PRIDE, by Charles T. Manners............
No. 9—THE WIDOW'S WAGER, by Rose Ashleigh............
No. 8—WILL SHE WIN? by Emma Garrison Jones............
No. 7—GRATIA'S TRIALS, by Lucy Randall Comfort............
No. 6—A STORMY WEDDING, by Mrs. Mary E. Bryan............
No. 5—BRUNETTE AND BLONDE, by Mrs. Alex. McVeigh Miller............
No. 4—BONNY JEAN, by Mrs. E. Burke Collins............
No. 3—VELLA VERNELL; or, An Amazing Marriage, by Mrs. Sumner Hayden............
No. 2—A WEDDED WIDOW, by T. W. Hanshew............
No. 1—THE SENATOR'S BRIDE, by Mrs. Alex. McVeigh Miller............

These popular books are large type editions, well printed, well bound, a in handsome covers. For sale by all Booksellers and Newsdealers; or se *postage free*, on receipt of price, 25 cents each, by the publishers,

STREET & SMITH,

P. O Box 2784.   25 to 31 Rose Street, New Yo

CPSIA information can be obtained
at www.ICGtesting.com
Printed in the USA
BVHW041127040219
539410BV00006B/136/P